RATFACE

RATFACE

by Garry Disher

Ticknor & Fields Books for Young Readers

NEW YORK 1994

Copyright © 1993 by Garry Disher

First American edition 1994 published by
Ticknor & Fields Books for Young Readers
A Houghton Mifflin company, 215 Park Avenue South,
New York, New York 10003.

First published in Australia by Angus & Robertson,
an imprint of HarperCollins Publishers Pty Limited,
Sydney, Australia 1993.

Manufactured in the United States of America
The text of this book is set in 12 point Caledonia
BP 10 9 8 7 6 5 4 3 2 1

Library of Congress Cataloging-in-Publication Data
Disher, Garry.
Ratface / by Garry Disher.—1st American ed.   p.   cm.
"First published in Australia by Angus & Robertson . . . 1993"—T.p.
verso.
Summary: A teenage boy and girl attempt to escape from a racist cult
known as the White League.
ISBN 0-395-69451-5
[1. Cults—Fiction.   2. White supremacy movements—Fiction.
3. Prejudices—Fiction.   4. Racism—Fiction.   5. Orphans—Fiction.]
I. Title.   II. Title: Ratface.
PZ7.D6228Rat   1994
[Fic]—dc20   93-48131   CIP   AC

RATFACE

1

IT STARTED with the reporter.

Max was the first to see her. He was sitting in a patch of morning sunlight on the back steps, drowsily polishing Slinger's boots and Moaner's shoes, when a movement at the edge of the forest caught his attention. He looked up. Nothing. He must have imagined it. He shrugged and worked the shoebrush again.

Saturday tomorrow. The start of another gloomy Ratface Weekend. Max shook off the feeling, telling himself to enjoy the mild mountain air, the warm wooden smells of the veranda rails and steps baking the autumn sunlight.

Again there was that movement at the edge of the forest. This time he put down his brush and stood up, peering intently. A young woman was standing among the pine trees. She was about thirty meters away, a hazy outline in the filtered sunlight. He could sense tension in her, as if she was aware that she was trespassing.

Max knew that he should do something. He should tell Slinger and Moaner. They'd chase the woman off the property.

He looked left and right. There was no one else around. He didn't know where Slinger and Moaner were. That left Christina. She was chopping wood behind the house. She'd know what to do—she was not afraid of anyone or anything.

He looked at the young woman again—and froze. She was beckoning to him.

He'd been warned that this might happen. Ratface, Slinger, Moaner—they all said to beware of strangers: strangers meant harm to the White League.

At that moment, Christina appeared, stamping up the veranda steps with an armful of firewood. There were bark chips on her tunic and she looked flushed and irritable.

"Hard at work?" she asked sarcastically, dumping the wood into the box next to the back door.

Max blushed. Christina was fourteen, older than him by six months, and lately he had found himself sneaking admiring looks at her, as if he had never noticed her lively face and tossing hair before. He badly wanted her to show the same sort of interest in him. Instead, she lashed out at him.

Touching her arm before she could say anything else, he pointed toward the forest. "Look."

Christina's mood altered instantly. She stepped up to the veranda railing, intrigued. "Who is she?"

"Don't know."

"She's waving to us. Let's go and see what she wants."

Max's face creased in worry. Typical Christina—act first, think later. "We should tell Slinger and Moaner," he said.

Christina curled her lip at him. "You're such a goody-goody."

She jumped to the ground and strode across the lawn, tall, flashing, and scornful, her hair streaming behind her. Max sighed. He'd better go with her. Who knew what sort of trouble she might get them into? Besides, he was curious, too.

He caught up to her and together they approached the stranger, who stepped back as they got closer. She wore red jeans and a white shirt and carried a leather satchel over her shoulder. She looked anxious, but then smiled. "Hello."

Together, they responded warily: "Hello."

"I'm Gillian," the woman said. "I'm a reporter. I'd like to ask you some questions."

She had a soft, mild voice. Her smile reassured Max. But in talking to her, he and Christina were disobeying instructions, and he felt guilty about that. "Questions about what?" he asked cautiously.

Instead of replying, Gillian opened her satchel. "Do you recognize this woman?"

She held out a photograph. It was a head-and-shoulders shot of a haughty woman with stiff, fair hair.

"That's the Leader," Christina said.

"Of the White League?"

"Yes."

"Do you know her name?"

"No."

"She calls herself Dorothea Langley-Hall, but her real name is Doris Higgs," Gillian said, rummaging in her satchel again. She took out a newspaper clipping and offered it to Max and Christina without further comment.

They stood shoulder to shoulder, peering at it. "The Good Life," the headline said. Under it was a fuzzy photograph of a long, black limousine. The caption read: "Dorothea Langley-Hall, wanted by police in connection with fraud and tax evasion charges, pictured this week outside her luxury home on millionaires' row in Buenos Aires."

Max looked up at Gillian, troubled and confused. He didn't know what fraud and tax evasion were. He'd never heard of Buenos Aires. What did Gillian want with them? "I don't understand," he said.

"Neither do I," said Christina.

"You are White League children, is that correct?" Gillian asked.

"Yes."

Gillian's voice grew cool and flat. "Mrs. Langley-Hall, the woman you call the Leader, is nothing but a common criminal. She tricked gullible people into investing millions of dollars in the White League, then ran off with it all. She's a fake. If she ever comes back here to Australia, she'll be jailed."

Max stepped back. The words were like physical blows. He couldn't make sense of them. For as long as he could remember, he'd been taught to revere the Leader. Every evening they listened to tapes of her speeches.

"It's not true," he said. "You're trying to trick us."

He looked around to see if Slinger or Moaner were anywhere in sight. They weren't. He saw only the long, low house and the sheds in the clearing, the fruit trees, and the vegetable gardens. There was no wind. The only noise was the faint muttering of the diesel engine that generated their electricity. The little farm looked peaceful and uncomplicated in the morning sunlight. He turned to Gillian again. "You're mistaken," he said. "The Leader represents God in a godless world."

Only an outsider could doubt that. Max had never met the Leader, but in his mind's eye she was strong, kind, and wise, dressed in white, a shimmering light around her. "You're mistaken," he repeated.

Gillian smiled gently at him. She took a bundle of newspaper clippings from her satchel and handed half to him, half to Christina. "See for yourselves."

During the next couple of minutes, Max and

Christina pored over the clippings. Max felt dazed. One clipping after another gave him a different perspective on the Leader. The light that shone around her began to fade a little, and he couldn't stop it. He didn't want to believe that the Leader was ordinary and human after all—a fake, in fact; a criminal—but that is what the newspapers said.

Christina looked up first. "It says here that the Leader's been in jail before."

Gillian nodded. "Many years ago she ran something similar to the White League in America. She set up family cells in isolated areas. She also got ordinary people to donate lots of money. She spent a year in prison in California."

Max still didn't understand. "Does that mean we'll be jailed, too?"

"Of course not. You've been tricked, that's all."

Max looked at Christina, but she ignored him. She didn't look shocked; she was smiling slightly and nodding her head. Looking at the notebook in Gillian's hands, she asked, "What do you want to know?"

"Perhaps your names first."

"I'm Christina, and this is Max."

"Who else lives here besides you two?"

Christina grinned. "Slinger and Moaner."

Gillian looked at her and laughed. "Slinger and Moaner?"

"That's what we call them behind their backs. Slinger we're supposed to call Father, and Moaner we're supposed to call Mother."

Gillian scribbled in her notebook. Max felt left out. Christina was doing all the talking. He said, "There are families like us all through the hills. The White League."

Gillian turned to him and smiled. "Do you know them?"

"Some of them. We have meetings."

"What about?"

Christina snorted. "The usual rubbish."

Max turned on her angrily. "Don't say that."

"Says who?" she flashed back.

"It's not right," he said stubbornly.

There were times when she confused and upset him. According to the White League, he was special and so was she. Those outside the fold—like the reporter, Gillian—led selfish, worthless lives, obsessed with material things. Spiritually they were shallow. Their schools had made them doubters and atheists. They were weak, extending rights and friendship to blacks and Asians. Max was burning to say all this to Gillian, to get her to believe, but he knew that Christina would only mock him, just as she mocked the Leader's speeches. He took a deep breath and made himself be calm.

Gillian's head was bowed as she wrote again. She had black hair, very black. Max was fascinated by it. He wanted to reach out and see what it felt like. His own hair seemed to cling to his head in tight, surprised curls. Like Christina's, it was pale and bleached in color. Everyone in the League had white or blond hair.

Gillian took out another photograph. "Do you know this man?"

Max and Christina looked. "Ratface."

Gillian grinned again. She pointed her pen at Christina. "I bet you were the one who made up these names."

Christina shrugged. "We have to do something for fun around here."

"What are you supposed to call him?"

"Uncle."

"What's he done?" asked Max. "Is he in trouble, too?"

"What do you think?" Gillian asked. "Do you think he's committed any crimes?"

The suggestion seemed outrageous to Max. Uncle a criminal? Impossible. Uncle was scary, but only because he had to keep the White League forever vigilant against the outside world. "Impossible," he said firmly.

"Nevertheless," Gillian said, "he's a senior figure in the White League, so I'd like to ask him what he intends to do now that your Leader has run off with all the League's money. Do you see him very often?"

"Once a month," Christina said. "We call them Ratface Weekends. He's coming tomorrow."

"Great," Gillian said.

She seemed to be very pleased with herself, which troubled Max. It had been drummed into them never to reveal details about the White League to strangers.

"We have to go," he said.

He was ignored. Christina was watching Gillian intently. Her expression was complicated—excited and curious, but also admiring, as if Gillian had opened a door into a new, more desirable world. Max felt uneasy.

"This next question is more personal," Gillian said. "Can you tell me how you came to be here?"

"My parents died when I was little," Max said, "so I was adopted."

"He's been here the longest," Christina said. "I came here when I was nine." She went on to explain that she'd been raised in the city by a family who had had links with the White League. Then, five years ago, she had been sent here, to this farm in the hills. "I don't know anything about my mother or father." She blinked away sudden tears. "I think they died."

Gillian was watching both of them oddly. She opened her mouth as if to say something, then closed it again.

"Okay. Next question. What can you tell me about the teachings of the White League?"

Max could see from the sour look on Christina's face that she was about to say something critical. He said quickly: "We are the Supreme Line. One day we will lead the world out of the mess it's in."

"I see," Gillian said. There was a hint of sarcasm in her voice.

"People have let themselves get too comfortable," Max went on. "They lack ambition, they've lost sight of right and wrong, they mix with inferior races. But the League has reached a higher stage of consciousness. When the Great Catastrophe happens, we will be ready to step in and establish order."

He knew all this from the Leader's lecture tapes. His belief was absolute.

Gillian grinned nastily at him. "What if I were to tell you that everything the White League preaches is untrue? You do not belong to a Supreme Line of people. You are just like everyone else, and your Leader—well, she's the sort of person who manipulates people and feeds them lies."

Max felt his heart pounding. They had been warned about people like Gillian. Every Ratface Weekend it was drilled into them that there were people outside the League who wanted to destroy it and who would use any kind of trick to do so. "You're lying," he said hotly. Even Christina was staring.

Gillian waved the newspaper clippings in his face: "Look at the Leader's face. She's sixty years old but she looks thirty-five. Do you know why? She's had cosmetic surgery, that's why. She's a vain, selfish woman who enjoys every luxury the outside world has to offer while poor suckers like you deny yourselves everything. Do you really think she wants to live as you do? Come on, Max. Don't let her pull the wool over your eyes."

The attack was shocking. Christina seemed

excited again, but Max was devastated. Without the Leader, without the White League, who was he? What did he have? Nothing, nothing.

"Shut up." Tears pricked his eyes. "Just you shut up." He heard the League's words in his head, and said them aloud: "We are Supreme and you are Nothing."

At that moment, a voice called to them: "What's going on? Who are you talking to?"

Max turned around. Slinger was watching them, a tense, stooped, lanky shape on the veranda stairs. Moaner joined him.

"I'd better go," Gillian said, stepping back from them.

Slinger's voice swelled with anger. "You! Get away from those children. Get off this property before I call the police."

"There's more," Gillian whispered. "Same time, same place tomorrow."

2

$I\,\scriptsize{T}$ $\scriptsize{WAS}$ $\scriptsize{CLEAR}$ to Christina that the next few hours were going to be unbearable. One look at the faces of Slinger and Moaner told her that. She was with Max in the cold, dim kitchen, sitting in the stiff wooden chairs, enduring a barrage of questions. The man they called Father and the woman they called Mother were angry, fearful, and querulous.

"Who was that woman?" they wanted to know. "What did she want? What did you tell her?"

"Nothing," Christina muttered.

Slinger was incredulous. "Nothing? Don't lie."

Christina looked across at Max, narrowing her eyes warningly at him: *Don't tell them anything.* It didn't work. He was still upset. He wanted reassurance that Gillian should not be believed. Avoiding her gaze, he looked up and said, "She's a reporter. She wanted to know about the League."

"Oh dear," Moaner said. Her hands began to twist with the washing motions they made whenever she was nervous.

Slinger leaned his mournful face close to Max. "What did you tell her?"

"We said—"

Christina stood up, knocking her chair over. "It doesn't matter what we told her, it's what *she* told *us* that matters."

Moaner's hands were busy, busy. She was a plump woman with pale skin. Normally she looked patient and calm. Now she looked anxious. "What did she tell you?"

Christina folded her arms. "All about the Leader."

Slinger's shoulders slumped a little. He turned to look out at the forest beyond the window. "Soon the place will be swarming with reporters," he muttered. He turned back to them again. "Exactly what did she tell you about the Leader?"

Christina was enjoying this. Slinger and Moaner were generally kind, but they could be stuffy. She'd never seen them this emotional about anything before. Watching their faces for a reaction, she said, "You've all been fooled. The Leader is just a fake, a criminal. She ran off with all the League's money."

Slinger and Moaner looked saddened rather than surprised. They already know, Christina realized.

They've been trying to keep it from us. She paused, formulating another bombshell. "We were also told that everything you've been teaching us is rubbish." She laughed harshly. "That's what I've been thinking all along."

In fact, she hadn't been thinking that—at least, not before meeting Gillian. But she had been feeling restless and dissatisfied. Every minute of every day someone was telling her what to do and what to think, and she hated it. Now, according to Gillian, it was all lies.

"All lies," she said.

Slinger groaned, his shoulders slumping further. Moaner collapsed into a chair.

Slinger recovered first. "I'm surprised at you," he said, "believing in the claims of a complete stranger."

"The future is in our hands," said Moaner. "The League is growing stronger day by day here in the mountains, protected from the influences that would weaken the Line if we lived among people on the outside."

Christina had heard all this before. She sighed heavily, rolled her eyes, folded her arms, tapped her foot—her way of telling Slinger and Moaner that she wasn't listening.

"Stop that," Slinger said. "Pick up your chair and sit down."

Christina flared at him. "Not till you explain why the Leader ran off with the League's money."

Got you, she thought, noting the doubt and confusion on his face.

"There's a perfectly logical explanation," Slinger said finally. "Newspapers are always trying to damage the reputations of people with forward-thinking ideas."

Christina glanced at Max for help. He was sitting miserably in his chair, his eyes fixed on the tabletop. Generally she liked to look at him. He had the kind of face that she wished she had—high cheekbones, a sensitive mouth, a well-shaped head on a slender neck. But right now he irritated her. He hated conflict; she thrived on it. He was naive and accepting; she liked to prod and pry into things. She would have to do this alone.

"The Leader cheated people in America and was jailed for it," she snapped. "Are you saying the newspapers lied?"

Slinger shifted awkwardly. "Yes," he said. He sounded doubtful.

"Then why hasn't the Leader defended herself? Why hasn't she challenged them? Why did she run away?"

Moaner interrupted them. "Uncle visits tomorrow. I'm sure he'll explain it to us."

Christina opened her mouth to argue again, then stopped abruptly. She had enjoyed pushing Slinger and Moaner, sensing their uncertainty, hoping to get them to admit to doubts about the Leader, but now she felt guilty. They were timid people who derived strength from the White League. And they had always treated her kindly. Perhaps she should be attacking the teachings of the League, not Slinger and Moaner, but she didn't know how.

She picked up her chair and sat down. "I hate it when Uncle comes," she mumbled. "He's always telling us what to think and do. He's turning us into puppets. We're just like blocks of wood."

"But he's the Leader's deputy," said Slinger gently. "He knows best."

"He takes all the fun out of life," Christina said. She had an image of him in her mind. She called him Ratface because his face was narrow and pinched, like a rodent's. "I hate the way he checks up on us. You two were the ones chosen to prepare us for the future. We don't need Uncle poking his nose in as well."

Then anger stirred inside her again. "I hate the way you agree with everything he says and does. You should stand up to him sometimes."

Come on, Max, she thought. Help me. She looked at him. He was watching her, half shocked, half admiring. There were times when she felt close to him and times like now, when she wanted to shake him. "What do you think, Max?"

Max blushed. He stammered. It's no good, Christina thought. He's never known anything but the League. It would take something huge to change him.

Slinger interrupted, clapping his hands together

sharply. "Enough of this. We've all got chores to do. I suggest we wait till tomorrow and hear what Uncle has to say. Max, come with me. Christina, help Mother."

Max and Slinger left the room. After a moment of awkward silence, Moaner stood up and slid her chair under the table. Like Christina, she wore a simple cotton tunic, the White League uniform for women. She brushed invisible crumbs from it. "Perhaps we can do some cooking, dear."

Christina sighed. It was always dark and cold in the kitchen. Sacks of nuts and seeds sat in the corners of the room. Jars of lentils and dried fruit stood on the shelves and benches. Beans were soaking in a bowl of water, and a clump of unappetizing-looking leaves waited on the chopping board. "Yes, Mother."

She sounded obedient, but she was thinking of tomorrow and talking to Gillian again.

3

CHRISTINA opened her eyes. It was morning; she could hear the complicated songs of the magpies in the forest, but she wasn't interested in the magpies. She was interested in the dream that she'd just woken from.

It was a familiar dream. It occurred at least once a week, and she hated the lonely, empty mood it left her in. She dreamed she was rowing a small boat across a limitless ocean. Her destination was a tiny figure on a tiny speck of land on the far horizon. The figure was making sad, imploring gestures, as if beseeching her to hurry, telling her that time was running out and they might never be reunited. But no matter how vigorously Christina rowed, the island got no closer. In fact, it seemed to retreat until it vanished. And the oars were heavy, heavy. It was the same dream, except this time Christina woke up knowing that the tiny, beckoning figure was her mother.

She found herself thinking of the city, of her life there before she was brought here to the farm. After five years, she had forgotten many of the details, but she did remember that there had always been a sense of promise then, as if she might one day meet interesting people or do interesting things. She'd been living with a pleasant, ordinary family at the time, distant cousins of the Leader. Then Ratface had come into their lives and persuaded them to give her up to the White League, to be raised by Slinger and Moaner. She'd never forgiven him for it. She did her chores, she listened to the Leader's lecture tapes, but at her core she had kept a spark of bitterness and doubt.

And now that spark had been kindled. Gillian would help her make sense of things.

She got up feeling unsettled and depressed. She did not whistle in the shower. She did not answer when Max, Slinger, and Moaner wished her good morning, and her participation in the daily prayer and exercise rituals was spiritless and automatic.

Breakfast was milk poured over a bowl of mixed grains and dried fruit, all produced on the farm, together with toast made from the bread that Max liked to bake. She picked at everything. It was tasteless.

Slinger leaned toward her. "Christina, you're not to dwell on what happened yesterday. Remember the Leader's words and draw strength from them."

Christina looked at him and blinked. She experienced a curious sensation of detachment. She observed his hollow-cheeked face, the pores in his nose, the chewing motions of his jaw, his plain, dust-colored League uniform of matching shirt and trousers, and she felt that he wasn't a person but a familiar object. She looked at Moaner. There didn't seem to be anybody inside Moaner's kindly exterior either. She looked at Max. Max blushed immediately, as if she'd caught his secret thoughts. She blinked again and the world was back to normal.

But something had changed. She felt restless, curious to know more about the White League and about the lives of people outside it. She wanted answers, and she intended to get them from Gillian later that morning.

Slinger seemed to know what she was thinking. "No more talking to strangers, you two. Is that understood?"

"Yes, Father," Christina said brightly.

"We've got a lot of work to do before Uncle arrives," Slinger continued. "Christina, I want you to finish staking the tomato plants."

"Yes, Father."

"Max, I want you to drive while I feed the cattle."

Max grinned. "Yes, Father."

He enjoyed driving the little pick-up truck, even

if all he ever did was bump it across the back paddock in low gear once a week. Christina, watching the anxiety leave his face, felt very alone.

She was about to get up from the table when Moaner's plump hands pressed down on her shoulders. She heard breathing at the back of her head and felt fingers parting her hair. "It's time we bleached your hair, dear."

"Not again."

"Yes, my girl. There's too much brown showing. You know Uncle doesn't like to see that."

Christina scowled and accompanied Moaner to the bathroom. She leaned over the sink, with towels wrapped around her neck and shoulders, while Moaner bleached her hair. She hated it. The color looked unnatural, the chemicals stung her eyes, and she felt as if she were being turned into someone else, someone who wasn't her.

When it was over, Christina dried her hair in the sun, put on old shoes, and went into the vegetable garden at the side of the house. The air was clear, warm, and scented. She started work, bending and straightening among the tomato plants. The sun climbed above the trees. The diesel engine hummed in the generator shed. The main power line for the mountain districts passed near the farm, but the White League liked to be self-sufficient. "We won't have anything to do with governments," Ratface would say.

Christina worked for about thirty minutes, then,

checking the time on her watch, ran half-crouched to the edge of the forest.

"You came," Gillian said.

Today she was wearing a clinging black skirt, red tights, plum-colored lipstick, and yellow plastic earrings in the shape of parrots on a swing. A short leather jacket was draped over her shoulders. She looked cheerful and confident, with a dashing beauty that Christina envied.

"I can't stay long," Christina said. "We got into trouble yesterday."

"Where's Max?"

"Working."

Gillian frowned. "That's a pity. I needed to speak to both of you today."

Then she did an odd thing. She turned around, looked searchingly back among the trees, and gave a brief nod. She turned to Christina again and took her by the elbow. "Why don't we stand over here, where the light's a bit brighter," she said.

Christina glanced nervously at the house. No one was around. She let herself be guided to a clearing where the sun penetrated through a gap in the trees. Gillian was fussy about where they should position themselves. She also insisted on standing next to Christina. Finally she made adjustments to an unusual pin on her lapel, fumbled in the bag hanging from her shoulder, and said, in a loud, clipped voice:

"The Leader has fled overseas, wanted by the

police. The teachings of the White League have been shown to be dangerously racist, narrow, and undemocratic. How do you react to that?"

Christina was perplexed by Gillian's manner. She'd come to her for answers, not questions. "It's a bit much to take in," she said after a while. "I don't understand what's going on."

"You and the boy, Max, have been here for several years?"

"Yes."

"Are you well treated?"

"Yes."

This answer didn't seem to satisfy Gillian. "What about your education?" she asked. "What sort of things are you taught?"

"Mother gives us lessons every day."

"What sort of lessons?"

Christina shrugged. Why was Gillian asking all these stupid questions? "Reading, writing, math, science."

"Anything else?"

"We learn about the troubles of the world, how we need people who are strong and pure to lead us in the future because we've allowed ourselves to grow weak," answered Christina automatically. She paused, irritated with herself for repeating the words of the Leader. "What did you mean yesterday when—"

"Both you and Max are adopted?" Gillian broke in.

Christina frowned. Gillian already knew that. "Yes."

Then Gillian said the most shocking thing of all. "Now that you know the White League is built on lies," she said, "I expect you'll want to get out and look for your real mother?"

Christina gasped. "My real mother?"

"I'm sorry, I didn't mean to startle you," Gillian said. She didn't look very sorry. "According to my research, the White League has been bending the adoption laws. Destitute young mothers in the city have been persuaded to give their children up for adoption. False papers have been drawn up. The League badly needs all the children it can get to be raised as the Master Race of the future."

Christina couldn't manage her voice very well. She swallowed, coughed, swallowed again. "You mean my mother's alive?"

"I don't know," Gillian said, "but there's a good chance that she is. The law now makes it easier for adoptees to track down their real mothers, and the father, if he's known."

"What about Max's mother?"

"It's possible she's alive, too. I think you were told you were orphans so that you wouldn't think about your real parents and would become loyal to the League."

Christina was silent. Gillian watched her. "I might be wrong. You must be prepared for that."

Christina looked at her helplessly. "What now? What should I do? What about Max?"

"I would like to speak to you both in a few days," Gillian said. She looked thoughtfully at Christina. "Have you ever considered escaping from here? Perhaps I could help you."

All the time they'd been speaking, Gillian had been facing Christina sometimes, a spot among the trees other times. Christina watched her gaze shift again. Then she heard it: a faint metallic noise and the sounds of foliage being disturbed. She'd been half-aware of these sounds for a while.

She was about to say something when Gillian stiffened and looked toward the house. "You've got visitors."

Christina looked. Two cars were creeping along the driveway. The first car was familiar to her. She saw it stop by the front door. Ratface got out and seemed to look at her, even though she was sure she couldn't be seen.

The second car was unfamiliar, but its driver wasn't. He was a tall, genial, angular man, who got out of his car buttoning his uniform jacket. Sergeant Hanley. He sometimes attended White League meetings. Slinger and Moaner must have telephoned Ratface about what happened yesterday, Christina thought, and Ratface decided to bring the policeman. She saw Sergeant Hanley place his uniform cap firmly on his head and stand next to Ratface. Then the two men began to approach the trees.

Christina reached out and clutched Gillian's arm. *"Take me with you."*

But Gillian jerked away and swore viciously, spitting her words. "A cop," she said.

Christina was stunned by this sudden, ugly change. She watched as Gillian wheeled around, crossed the little clearing, and said, facing the trees, "Quick, before he nabs us."

A young man emerged from the trees. He wore earrings and a ponytail, and he was struggling with black boxes, cables, and a video camera on a tripod.

"Quick," Gillian repeated, unclipping the pin on her lapel. A slender black wire was attached to it. A microphone.

Tears of betrayal and anger filled Christina's eyes. "You tricked me," she said. "You tricked me."

She burst away and ran toward the house. For the first time in her life, she was glad to see Ratface.

4

SLINGER TOSSED the last of the hay to the snorting, liquid-eyed cattle and thumped on the roof of the truck, signaling Max to stop. Max carefully put the gear lever into neutral, drew on the hand brake, and slid across to the passenger seat. He would have loved to drive back to the sheds, an opportunity to try changing gears, but he knew that Slinger would never allow it.

Slinger got into the driver's seat. "You did very well. Slow and smooth, none of your usual jerks."

Slinger's voice was unusually kind and animated. Perhaps he feels bad about all the arguments yesterday, Max thought.

"We'd better get back," Slinger said. "I saw a couple of cars turn into our driveway."

They parked the truck next to the car in the shed, walked companionably back across the yard, and found everything in an uproar—Sergeant Hanley was crashing along the edge of the forest searching among the trees. Christina and Moaner were looking tense and fearful while Ratface berated them in a low, bitter voice.

As they drew closer, Ratface looked up. "I hold you responsible," he snarled, pointing at Slinger. "This young lady"—he indicated Christina—"went and talked to the reporter again, the moment your back was turned."

They all looked at Slinger. Max felt sorry for him. Slinger's long face grew longer, his shoulders hunched protectively. "I didn't think she'd come a second time."

"Didn't think, didn't think," Ratface said. "That's your main trouble. There are going to be some changes around here."

Then his gaze lingered on Max. Max swallowed, his heart clenching. He'd always been afraid of the man they called Uncle. Ratface was slight, quick-moving, almost bald. No one would look twice at him in the street, but his eyes gave him away. They were hypnotic, compelling, glittering with intelligence. Max felt them probing him, finding his guilt and weaknesses. I'll never be able to please him, he thought, and I'll never be able to hide anything from him. He blushed and looked away.

"League conference," Ratface said. "Wait for me in the lesson room."

He strode away to talk to Sergeant Hanley. "You heard him, children," Moaner said. "We'll join you in a minute."

Christina had been tense and silent, but now she seemed to recover her spirits. She clasped Max's fingers. "Come on, Max."

He let himself be pulled into the house. Her hand felt hot. Her grip was tight, as if she was relieved to be with him, someone closer to herself than the large, blundering, troubled adults. He wanted to hug her.

The lesson room was at the back of the house. A map of the world hung on one wall, a clean blackboard on another. There were no pictures or ornaments, only a shelf of dull, heavy books. The curtains were closed. They had been like that since a Ratface Weekend five years earlier, when Ratface had caught Christina gazing out of the window.

They sat at their plain wooden desks. "What happened?" Max asked. "Did you see Gillian?"

"I certainly did. She tricked me."

"How?"

"She was secretly filming me. She wanted you to be there, too."

"Filming you?"

"Yes," Christina said. "Ratface told me about her. Apparently she likes to dig up dirt on people. He said she'll sell the interview to a television station."

There was a television set in the house, but they were allowed to watch only nature programs. Max didn't know what it would mean for Christina to be on television. He looked at her, bewildered.

"Close your mouth or you'll catch flies," she snapped.

Max looked away. Why was she always like that? He heard a car being driven away, and then footsteps in the corridor.

Ratface entered first, followed by Slinger and Moaner, who sat at the remaining desks. Max tried to feel resigned. He hated Ratface's lessons. Moaner's were slow and relaxed—art, reading, and hikes, with examples from nature used to demonstrate laws of science and mathematics. But Ratface taught from little books illustrated with comic strips that warned of the influences, tricks, and false promises that could weaken the purity of the Master Race. The drawings weren't very good.

Today was different. He stood at the blackboard and fixed his eyes on each of them in turn. When he finally spoke, his voice was low and chilling. "We face a grave crisis."

No one spoke. They all waited.

"As you know, the Leader had been forced to flee. The newspapers are trying to discredit her and the League."

Max couldn't stop himself. "The lady told us the Leader's a criminal, that she stole all the League's money."

He heard sharp intakes of breath from Slinger and Moaner. Too late, he realized that his interruption must have sounded like a criticism or a challenge. He sunk lower in his seat.

A stillness came over Ratface. His eyes fixed on Max, and Max stared back, unable to resist their force. He could scarcely swallow, scarcely breathe. He imagined Ratface's hands clamped around his neck, the long, pale, restless fingers tightening. Then Ratface moved. Slowly, slowly, he came across the room. Max closed his eyes helplessly.

But Ratface went through one of the sudden mood reversals that always kept Max feeling unsettled and insecure around him. Ratface's tone was mild, his hands gentle on Max's shoulders. "Don't you see, Max?" he asked. "It's all part of the plot to weaken us. In fact," he said, returning to the front of the room, "the reason the Leader took large sums with her overseas is quite simple—she intends to further the League's aims in other countries. When the Great Catastrophe occurs, the League will be prepared. In her absence, I will carry on her work here."

Then Christina spoke. Her voice was troubled. "The reporter made fun of the League's ideas."

Ratface smiled. "The reporter tricked you, remember. Can you really believe anyone who'd do that to you?"

Christina bowed her head. "No," she muttered.

"No," Ratface said. "We in the League lead a simple life, but it's a good life. No contaminating influences from the wider world. You children of the White League are our only hope. You have been reborn in white light and perfect joy. What is the Key?"

Automatically they all chanted, "We are the custodians of the League's work for future generations."

Ratface beamed.

5

THAT LOOKED LIKE the end of the matter, but during the night Max was awoken by something he couldn't at first identify. He checked his watch: midnight. He'd been half-awake for some time. Now that he was fully awake, he realized that he could hear voices, low, insistent, continuous. He got out of bed and padded across to his bedroom door. The adults were arguing in the sitting room.

He slipped out and edged along the wall of the corridor. The sitting room door was shut, and so he had to put his ear to it before he could distinguish meaning in the buzz of voices.

"But what if we *have* been tricked?"

Moaner's voice. Max could picture her hands twisting and turning.

"Impossible."

Ratface.

"But the newspapers can't be entirely wrong about the Leader."

Slinger.

"The Leader's been under considerable pressure," Ratface replied. "She's been affected by her proximity to undesirable practices in the outside world. It finally got to be too much for her and she made mistakes. That doesn't mean we abandon the cause of the White League."

"I'm worried about the children," Moaner said. "The reporter might have told them about the adoptions."

"Then you must be extra-vigilant from now on. Stress the teachings of the League at every opportunity. Never let the children out of your sight. Don't let them talk to strangers. Understood?"

There was a low murmur in response.

"Anyway," Ratface continued, "by this time next week all League properties will be impenetrable."

What did Ratface mean by that? And what had Moaner been saying about adoptions? Max strained to hear, but the three voices dropped. He turned away and crept back along the corridor.

As he was passing Christina's door, she opened it and whispered, "What's going on?"

"Shh," Max said. He glanced back down the corridor, then pushed past Christina into her room. She was dressed in a vast cotton nightgown that had once belonged to Moaner. Hunched over and shivering, she climbed back into her bed and said, "Sit here and tell me what's going on."

Max perched on the edge of the bed, disturbed by her warmth and proximity, her tousled hair and drowsy face. He wanted to climb in next to her and feel her shoulder against his. He wanted to put his arm around her. But would she welcome that? Confused, he pushed away his feelings and said, "I couldn't make sense of it. Ratface seemed to be admitting that the Leader had done something wrong after all. Then he said something was going to happen to all the League properties. Moaner said something about adoptions."

Christina had been propped up on one elbow. Now she slid down into the bed until only her head was showing on the pillow. She stared at the ceiling. "Gillian also said something about adoptions this morning."

"Gillian? You can't believe her. She tricked you."

"Yes, but what if she thought it was the only way she could get information? It doesn't mean that everything she said is untrue."

"It was still wrong of her. Ratface says no one on the outside can be trusted."

Christina sat up again, quivering with emotion. "Maybe it's Ratface we shouldn't trust. The League. Slinger and Moaner. Gillian told me our mothers could be alive."

Max stared at her. "Alive?"

"They might have given us up for adoption because they were young and couldn't manage."

"Why were we told they were dead?"

"So we wouldn't feel ties to anyone else, only the League."

"What about our fathers?"

Christina shrugged. "Maybe they ran out on our mothers. Maybe both parents didn't want us, or couldn't cope with us."

This was too much to take in. Max couldn't make sense of his feelings. If his mother was alive, what would she look like? What would his father look like? Would he be able to recognize them? Would he like them—or should he blame them for abandoning him? If he found them, would they want to have anything to do with him?

For the first time, blood ties mattered to him. He needed to know that someone existed whose flesh and blood were *his* flesh and blood.

Then Christina said, "I think Gillian wanted to set up an escape so she could film it. Too bad it didn't happen. I could be looking for my mother by now."

A powerful sensation of loss and rejection settled on Max. He didn't know what he would do if he was separated from Christina. The League was the only life he knew, and only Christina made it bearable. He feared the outside, feared that if he went with her she would soon leave him to make a life for herself.

How would he manage if that happened? Who would he trust? There was a huge difference between Christina and himself, he realized. Max felt that a part of him was missing, now that the Leader had been unmasked. He hated to think of Ratface filling up that space.

He didn't trust himself to speak. He muttered, "Good night," and made his way back to his room.

The next day the electric fence went up.

6

THE FENCE was high, grim, and unyielding. Taut strands of wire, charged with high-voltage current, were strung close together on white ceramic insulators fastened to three-meter-high black posts. The house, sheds, and adjacent land were completely enclosed. There were two gates: one forming the front entrance, the other leading to the outer farmland at the rear. Both gates were electrified and kept locked at all times.

"This fence will keep the world out," Ratface said. Christina came to believe otherwise. As the months went by, she grew convinced that it was there to keep her in.

On the surface, their lives went on as before, in a peaceful routine of farming, gardening, and lessons. Ratface continued to visit, carrying on the work of the League.

But feelings of constraint and unease settled on the community. Locks and keys defined their daily activities. There were locks on both gates, the telephone, the steering wheel of each vehicle, the fuse box on the back porch. The television set was thrown out. The only books and magazines allowed now were League publications. All others were incinerated. Life became even more spartan, marked by dim lights, indoctrination, and hard work.

The change in Ratface bothered Christina the most. He talked of finding new children for the League. He visited for longer periods and his influence persisted when he wasn't there. Ratface Weekends became three- or four-day periods of lectures, everyone shut in the lesson room for hours at a time.

The lectures were increasingly obscure and mystical. "Sing out the names of the lost ages!" Ratface would cry, his eyes wild, spit flying from his lips. "Discover your vast, glowing centers! Forge bridges to the warrior in yourself! Uncover the warrior codes of the universe, ready yourselves for the Great Catastrophe!"

"Gawd," Christina would mutter.

"Shh," Max would whisper, anxious to protect her from Ratface's wrath.

"Shh, yourself."

Moaner's hands were never still now, and Slinger looked sadder and older. Whenever they were kind to Max and Christina, they had an air of apology. Christina was frustrated with them. If they truly believed that Ratface was acting unreasonably, why couldn't they say so? Why couldn't they show a spark of independence instead of relying on Ratface and the White League for guidance in the way of things? Max was no help. All he ever did was watch her, sad and devoted.

Then one day Ratface wanted to change their names. "Max," he said, "you will now be known as Kenelm."

Max smiled uncertainly. "Kenelm?"

"It's Old English for 'defender of the kindred.' Christina, you will be known as Olwen, 'white footprints.' "

"Gawd," Christina said.

She knew what was happening. Ratface was trying to destroy their pasts, their old identities. She took Max aside. "Now listen," she said. "We'll use the new names when Ratface is around, but when we're alone we use our real names. Okay? We can't forget who we are. We can't let them change everything about us."

Max agreed. Even he thought that a name change was going too far.

Then one day Christina found herself saying, "I'm getting out of this place. I've had enough." She didn't know where the words had sprung from, but now that she'd said them, she believed them.

Max was helping her harvest the last of the corn. He glanced up, his face troubled. "How?"

"I'll find a way."

Max was silent for a moment. Then he asked, "Even if you did, where would you go?"

"The city."

Christina was watching Max closely. She saw him glance around at the compound, as if he was comparing life in it with life outside the fence. "What'll you do there?"

Christina could feel her confidence growing. "Look for my mother," she said immediately.

But she was going too fast for him. He looked lonely and dispirited. She grabbed his arm. "Come with me," she said urgently. "If the two of us work together we'll have a better chance of escaping and surviving on the outside."

Max's face worked in panic. "We'll get caught. They'll bring us back again."

"Stop being such a wet blanket."

"Shh," he said, "they'll hear us. You know I want to come. I just think we should talk it over first, that's all."

But Christina had gone too far for that. Her mind was made up. "Fine. You stay here, grow up to be like Slinger and Moaner. See if I care."

She got up, turned away, and strode into the house.

Now that she had voiced it, the idea of escaping to the outside began to dominate her life. Her dream returned more often. She felt restless, hungry for information about the outside world. The city seemed to draw her to it, although her memories of it were vague. She remembered the physical details—houses, cars, trains, stores, the people who had raised her—but that wasn't enough. She wanted to know what people thought and felt, how they got on with one another, why they were critical of the Leader and the White League.

If I'm going to survive on the outside, she thought, then I'll need to know these things. The question was how. The League's publications were no help. The telephone was locked. Besides, who would she talk to? Who would bother to listen to her story? She hovered near the perimeter fence sometimes, but Gillian never came back.

Only once did she learn something about life on the outside. Three or four times a year, Slinger would venture out of the compound to purchase bulk quantities of the foods they couldn't provide for themselves. After one of these shopping trips, Christina helped him to unpack a carton containing rice, sugar, and flour. She noticed a newspaper lining the bottom of the carton. Waiting until Slinger was bringing sacks of flour to the pantry, she removed the newspaper, folded it quickly, and slipped it inside her tunic.

Later that day she took it out. What she read perplexed her. The world seemed to be a disturbed place, full of conflict. No wonder some of the

League's family units lived in the hills, away from all the troubles. The headlines, photographs, and articles all seemed to clamor for her attention, describing a way of life she'd almost forgotten but which half beguiled, half repelled her now. Did people really own all those things? Did they dress like that? Did they hurt and kill one another? Was the air poisoned? Could you really have a baby at fourteen? How? What sort of world let people live in doorways or cardboard cartons, to starve or freeze? Would that happen to her if she escaped?

It's not going to be easy, she thought, starting a new life after being shut away for so long.

There was nothing about the White League or the Leader. Gillian's name didn't appear as the author of any of the articles.

She showed Max the newspaper, hoping to stir his interest. He read it hungrily enough, but after a while a disapproving frown developed on his face and she knew he'd swung back to his unquestioning acceptance of the League. "A society that has allowed itself to grow weak," he said stuffily. He stabbed his finger at a couple of the photographs. "Look at this! A black woman getting an award for writing a book! And this! Kids like us playing sports with Asian kids! It's not right."

Christina sighed. That's exactly what Ratface says, she thought.

She reread the article about the fourteen-year-old girl who had given birth to a baby, and thought with an ache about her own mother. She held on to a flickering hope that her mother was still alive, but all she knew of her was the dream image, the solitary figure on the distant shore. If only she could put a face, a voice, a body to the figure. What sort of unhappiness or bad luck had made her mother abandon her? What would they say if they happened to meet again? Christina thought that they would be accepting and forgiving of each other. Loving. Ratface spoke about love all the time, but his kind of love wasn't open and generous, it was closed and suspicious.

The days passed. It all seemed hopeless. Her resolve weakened and Max seemed relieved when she stopped talking about escape, about the world beyond the fence. They settled into a routine that might go on forever.

A Ratface Weekend changed everything.

It was seven o'clock on a Friday evening. A cold wind gusted outside. The table was set and they were waiting for Ratface to arrive. Slinger and Moaner seemed to be unusually tense. The dining room table was set for six people, not five, but Christina scarcely noticed, knowing that Ratface brought guests with him from time to time.

They heard the beeping of a horn. Slinger went outside. A series of metallic rattles and knocks told them that he had opened the gate. They heard a car drive in and heard Slinger close and lock the gate again. The back door banged shut and footsteps approached the dining room.

Christina had been picking at split ends with her fingernails while she waited. Now she looked up. Slinger and Ratface were entering the room. Flanked by them, holding their hands and looking fearfully at the dismal furniture and the strange people, was a child she'd never seen before. He was about seven years old, and he looked utterly lost.

"This is Arne, meaning 'eagle,' " Ratface said. He looked sharply at Max and Christina. "Come and say hello to your new brother."

7

THE LITTLE BOY stood between Slinger and Ratface as if hypnotized. His hair was long and dark; it would soon be cut short and dyed blond. He wore a red sweatsuit and white sneakers. He had been crying. Suddenly life came back into his face.

"My name is Stefan!" he yelled. "I keep telling you, don't call me Arne!"

"There, there," said Moaner, kneeling in front of him. "This is your home now."

"Your mother didn't want you. She didn't love you," Ratface said. His voice was low, goading, full of false concern. He looked especially narrow and pinched, more ratlike than ever.

Christina shot out of her chair. She was

trembling. "Stop it!" she shouted, and ran sobbing from the room.

Max felt his control slipping away. "Not again. You can't do this again."

Ratface turned to Slinger and Moaner and said, "Put Arne to bed now. I'll deal with this."

They left, taking the boy with them.

Max held his breath. First, Ratface turned to look at him. Then he began to advance across the room. Finally his gaunt face was close to Max's, his hands resting on Max's shoulders. Max cringed at the touch of those long, clean, pale fingers. His anger drained away, leaving him helpless.

Ratface's voice, when it came, was calm. "Sometimes I think that you and your sister don't listen. The League has saved and protected you. Mother and Father can't have children of their own, but the League has given them you and Olwen, and you have been given a good home." He shook his head, as if he were hurt and perplexed. "Have all our efforts been for nothing?"

Max swallowed, trying to find his voice. He felt confused, guilty. Had he been repaying kindness with ingratitude? "Sorry, Uncle."

The hands did not move. They were like talons on Max's shoulders. The voice went on hypnotically:

"We all love you and take care of you. Yet you and your sister seem very slow to learn. I thought you were doing so well, but I must have been mistaken, mustn't I?"

"Sorry, Uncle."

The fingers tightened. Ratface's eyes glittered. "But we won't have any more nonsense about Arne, will we?"

"No, Uncle,"

"And you will speak to your sister, won't you?"

"Christina never listens to me," Max said unhappily.

"What was that?" Ratface said, cupping his hand to his ear. "I didn't quite catch the name."

"Olwen," Max said. "I meant to say Olwen."

"You will speak to her, won't you?"

"Yes, Uncle."

"After all, you were the first. You must learn responsibility. What is the Key?"

"We are the custodians of the League's work for future generations," said Max automatically.

"Exactly. But have you let the Key guide you tonight?"

"No, Uncle."

"But you will from now on, won't you?"

"Yes, Uncle."

"Good night, Kenelm. I will see you again before I leave tomorrow."

"Good night, Uncle."

Ratface walked from the room. Max watched him go. He felt wretched and confused. He hated and feared Ratface, but felt guilty about disobeying him. He knew what Christina would say. She would say Ratface was crazy and dangerous, and if they didn't resist him they would end up like Slinger and Moaner, who were weak and under his influence. Also, she said, Slinger and Moaner were grateful to Ratface for giving them children. They would never challenge him.

Max waited for a while, miserable. He wished that he could blink his eyes and find the world rearranged. He would have more courage. He would be alone with Christina forever. No more Ratface, Slinger, Moaner. No more electric fence.

He walked down the dark corridor and into his bedroom. It was a dim, stark room. It had never held toys or pictures, only a chest of drawers, a heavy wardrobe, and two narrow beds.

But now it seemed to be full of people. Stefan was in the spare bed, crying softly. Slinger and Moaner sat by him on the edge of the bed, and Moaner was holding a candle and stroking his forehead. Ratface stood watching from the shadows.

"I want my mother," said the boy, trying to sit up.

"Here I am," Moaner said helplessly. "Try to go to sleep now."

"I want my real mother."

"Now, now," said Moaner. "You're safe and snug in bed, and when you wake up you'll have an exciting new home to explore."

"With sheds and a big garden," said Slinger. "Won't that be nice?"

His tone was anxious. He pulled nervously at

his earlobe. Moaner's hands were busy washing in the cold, dark air. A realization came unbidden to Max, as clear and certain as something Christina would say: Uncle has ruined their lives. He caught himself: *Ratface* has ruined their lives.

Stefan said, "Leave me alone." He turned his back on them and pulled the blanket over his head. Moaner patted him and stood up.

"Good night, Arne," she said. "Good night, Kenelm."

"Good night, Mother," Max said.

They left the room. Max undressed and put on his pajamas. He got into his cold bed. He always felt too cold in this house. He blew out the candle. "Good night, Arne," he said.

At once there was movement and a terrified wail from the other bed. "I want the light on. Don't turn out the light. Please put the light on."

Max fumbled for the matches and lit the candle. Stefan was sitting bolt upright, looking shocked and afraid.

"It's all right," said Max. "I'll leave it on till you fall asleep."

"No! Leave it on all night!"

"Okay, okay."

"I want my mother," said Stefan desolately. "Why hasn't she come to take me home?"

Max felt helpless. "Shh, Arne, go to sleep now."

"Stefan," said the boy, sobbing. "My name is Stefan." He fell back onto his pillow.

"Stefan," said Max.

"I want my mother. I want to go home. Where's my mother? Why doesn't she come?"

In despair, Max got out of bed and put his arm around the boy. "It's all right," he said. "Don't cry, Stefan. Try to go to sleep now."

"That man came and taked me away. My mother runned after the car."

Max felt a chill settle on him. He'd assumed that Stefan had been given up for adoption or recently orphaned, but Stefan was claiming he'd been kidnapped. Max groaned. That was wrong, wrong. You can't simply snatch a child from its mother whenever it suits you. What if that's what happened to me? he thought. Maybe I'm not an orphan. Maybe I was kidnapped, and my parents are still out there somewhere, crying for me.

Max felt weak suddenly. He sat on the edge of the bed, his mind whirling, old doubts and fears coming to the surface. Until now, he'd been able to keep them buried. The White League had done all his worrying and thinking for him. But Stefan's story was deeply unsettling. Max would have to do something.

He crossed to the door and opened it cautiously. Ratface sometimes slept badly when he stayed with them and prowled the house in the middle of the night. Max listened. Silence. Only the cold air and the endless dark of the corridor.

He hurried through the gloom to Christina's

door, opened it, rigid with fear, and slipped into her room. He crept to the bed.

"Wake up," he said, shaking her shoulder.

Christina woke immediately. "What's wrong? If Ratface catches you he'll take it out on both of us."

"It's that new kid," Max said. "He won't stop crying."

"I don't blame him."

"I think Ratface kidnapped him."

"Too bad," Christina said. "It's not my problem. I don't want to have anything more to do with this madhouse."

"Please, Christina. You've got to help me."

"Why? What help have you given me lately?"

"Come on, he's really upset."

Christina lay back on her pillow. After a pause, Max heard her voice, low and sad. "Are you sure he was kidnapped?"

"He said his mother chased the car." Max felt outrage welling up inside him. "That's wrong. What Ratface did is wrong."

Christina got out of bed and they sneaked back along the corridor. At one point, Max felt her bump against him. She felt warm and soft.

In the bedroom, Christina went to Stefan's bed and sat down. "It's all right," she said to him. "Max and I will look after you. We won't let them hurt you."

But Stefan's crying got louder. Christina picked him up and rocked him. She looked up at Max. "You know what we have to do, don't you," she said.

It was a statement, not a question. In the light of the candle she looked fierce and beautiful. She gave him courage.

"Yes, I know," he said.

"Soon?"

He nodded. "Soon."

8

RATFACE LEFT on Sunday afternoon. That evening, Max and Christina tried to question Slinger and Moaner about Stefan. "Was he kidnapped?" they asked. "Does his mother belong to the League? Does she know what happened to him?"

"Uncle wouldn't kidnap anybody," they replied.

Christina glanced at them sharply. They looked uncomfortable. She wanted to press them further— get them to admit their doubts so that she could drive a wedge between them and Ratface—but they changed the subject.

In the days that followed, Christina and Max spent as much time as possible with Stefan. They showed him around the compound, gave him simple chores to do, and read to him at bedtime.

When Slinger and Moaner were not around, they encouraged him to talk about himself. On the second day, Stefan relaxed enough to offer shy answers to their questions. He was seven years old, he told them, and he lived with his mother in the city.

Christina smiled at the boy's growing animation. "Now, can you tell me about the day the man picked you up in his car?"

A shadow passed over Stefan's face. He stopped speaking. Christina quickly talked about something else.

Two evenings later, Stefan said unexpectedly, "Have you got a Harvey?"

"A Harvey?" said Max. "What's a Harvey?"

"Harvey," said Stefan, cross and confused.

"Is Harvey your father?" Christina asked gently.

Stefan collapsed onto the floor. He went red in the face and snorted with laughter. "Harvey the tomcat."

Christina laughed too and lifted him off the floor. She danced a wild jig with him in the cheerless sitting room, shouting, "Harvey the tomcat!" until Moaner sidled in and took Stefan to the bathroom to bleach his hair.

After that, Slinger and Moaner were more vigilant. They kept Stefan in their company for hours at a time, teaching him about the League. Christina and Max were discouraged from talking to him, and were often discouraged from talking to each other. They knew what was happening: Slinger and

Moaner feared Ratface. Whenever troubled by doubts, they would look to the White League. It gave meaning to their lives. And serving the League meant serving Ratface: they didn't want to appear lax in his eyes.

The effect on Stefan was immediate. He stopped speaking, grew pale and listless, and cried at night. At mealtimes he picked at his food.

Max couldn't bear it. In an effort to cheer Stefan up, he made a cat from scraps of felt and black wool. It was a lumpy, soft, unraveling creature, which he named Harvey Two.

"Here, Stef," he said when it was finished. Stefan looked at it for a moment in alarm, then reached out, poked it, took it, and from that moment wouldn't be parted from it. But he changed little. He fretted. He was silent.

A few days later, Max and Christina found an opportunity to discuss their situation. They were weeding the garden with Slinger. When Slinger left them for a few minutes to fetch the wheelbarrow, Max watched him go, then asked, "Have you thought any more about escaping?"

Christina pulled up a thistle. It broke, coating her fingers with sap. "All the time. Have you?"

He nodded. "I think we have four main problems. First, to get over the electric fence or through the gate. Second, to get as far away as possible, before Slinger and Moaner discover we're missing, which means we should try to escape at night. Third, a lot of League families live in the area. We'll have to avoid them. Fourth, the city's a long way from here and it's going to be hard to find where Stefan lives."

"I can think of at least two more problems," Christina said. "We have to get out of the house itself, with Stefan, without waking Slinger and Moaner, and we'll have to carry things with us."

"What sort of things?"

"We might have to hide for a few days." She waved her arm to indicate the dense trees and steep mountains that surrounded them. "We'll need food, warm clothes, something to carry water in."

Max looked apprehensively past the electric fence, thinking about wild animals, rain, deep concealed pits, cliffs, treacherous rocks. It was going to be harder than he'd thought.

"There are other problems," Christina said. "It doesn't end with taking Stefan home. What about you and me? How are we going to live? Food, shelter, getting around, finding people we can trust— it's not going to be easy. And what if we can't find our own families? Or if we do, what if they don't want us?"

Max nodded miserably. He had been thinking those things, too. Suddenly Christina hissed, "Stop talking. Here comes Slinger." She reached for a weed and pulled it out.

Max said, quietly and rapidly, "Think about it and we'll compare notes again tomorrow."

But Slinger had heard him. "Compare notes?" he said, parking the wheelbarrow and kneeling beside him. "Now what can you two be comparing notes about, may I ask?"

He asked it shyly. He was a hesitant man who often stumbled over his words. Like Moaner, he seemed to enforce Ratface's edicts with an air of reluctance and apology.

Even so, Max stammered, unable to think of a reply.

Christina saved him, as she often did. She said, in her bored voice, "Just something Mother was talking about in the lesson today. Something we have to think about for tomorrow's lesson."

Slinger looked at her suspiciously but said nothing. Finally he stood up. "Kenelm, I want you to continue weeding. Olwen, come with me. I have another job for you."

The same thing happened the next day and the day after that. Just when they were about to discuss their plan, Slinger or Moaner interrupted or separated them.

They were luckier on the fourth morning. Their job was to wax the gloomy linoleum floors of the house, and for a few minutes they were uninterrupted while Slinger replaced a belt on the engine in the generator shed and Moaner ground herbs to make a medicine for Stefan. When she was sure the coast was clear, Christina took a scrap of paper from her sock and pushed it into Max's shirt pocket.

"Read it later," she whispered.

They kept on working. They could hear Moaner in the kitchen. She might come in at any moment.

After lunch Max went in search of eggs. The hens seemed to be the only relaxed creatures in the whole place. They roamed freely and had nothing to worry about except finding a secret place to roost. In the gardening shed, he took out Christina's note. She had scrawled a list:

> money
> strong shoes
> water bottle
> matches
> food
> warm clothes
> waterproof coats
> candles

He thought. Later that day he added to it:

> flashlight
> knife
> paper
> large sheets of plastic

He passed the list to Christina when they were washing the dishes that evening.

She cornered him by the woodpile the next morning. "What's this about plastic sheets?" she demanded.

"To put on damp ground or cover us when it rains."

"Gawd." She shook her head. "We can only manage simple, small things. I think we should forget about the plastic."

For a moment, Max thought that she was going to criticize everything on his list. She was in one of her impatient, bossy moods. But then she said warmly, "I hadn't thought of paper or a knife or a flashlight, though. Another thing we'll need is a tin opener."

"Will we be buying tinned food?"

She nodded. "Or stealing it."

Max was shocked. "Stealing it?"

"Yes. We have to be prepared to do things like that if necessary."

Max hoped it wouldn't come to that. "What about money?"

She smiled. "That's all taken care of."

"What do you mean?"

"For years I've been swiping a bit here and there—from their pockets, from the kitchen, from Moaner's bag, just in case. I've got plenty hidden away."

Max stared at her with admiration. She was even tougher than he'd thought.

"Next thing," she said. "The paper—is that to make fires with?"

"Yes. We'll take paper bags. That way we can carry things too."

60

"Knife?"

"I know where there's an old pocketknife of Slinger's," Max said.

"Great. Another thing we'll need is a map."

"There's one in the car."

"Matches?"

"That's easy," Max said. "Two boxes won't be missed."

"Water bottle?"

"There are those plastic bottles Slinger takes with him when he goes out to cut wood in the forest."

Then Moaner called. "Time for your lesson, children."

They made their way into the house. "It's exciting, don't you think?" Christina said.

"It's not a game. This is serious."

"Oh, I know. It's just that I feel so hopeful, and I haven't felt like that since they brought me here."

Max looked at her. He had been involved in himself and had not been paying attention to her. She always seemed so determined, he'd assumed she was never worried or unhappy. He felt closer to her.

9

IT WAS ANOTHER Ratface Weekend. On the night before Ratface's arrival, Max lay in the dark, listening to the coughing and the shallow, painful gasping in the bed next to him, and told himself, Soon, it must be soon.

"Stef?" he said aloud. "Are you all right?"

Stefan coughed a little and whimpered. He hadn't spoken to any of them for several days. His illness seemed to come and go. During the day he would be subdued, holding dully on to Harvey Two. At night he would thrash about as if in torment.

Max got out of bed and touched the boy's forehead. It felt damp and hot. He got back into bed and forced himself to concentrate. What was their biggest problem? Clearly, getting out. Once they were outside the fence they could move as fast as possible and hope for the best. They might be lucky, they might not. But the actual getting out would require more than luck.

Electricity—that was the key. Electricity controlled the gate. Electricity made the fence dangerous. The power supply came from a diesel generator connected to a bank of heavy-duty batteries. The engine was switched off during the day, but the batteries kept their charge through the night.

That was as far as he got before he fell asleep.

Ratface arrived early the next day. At once Max felt his new courage begin to drain away. Ratface seemed to fix a hard scrutiny on him the moment he entered the compound, and Max thought, He knows. He knows me inside and out. It's always going to be like this.

Max spent the morning avoiding Christina. He felt torn: she gave him strength, Ratface took it away.

She finally cornered him after lunch. He was sitting on the veranda steps, watching the three adults walking Stefan around the perimeter fence, when he heard her open and close the screen door behind him. He didn't turn around.

A moment later she sat next to him. "Stefan seems worse," she said firmly.

There was no avoiding it—she had her mind fixed on taking Stefan home to his mother. Max sighed. "His fever's getting worse."

"So we can't waste any more time."

Max burst out: "But how? How?"

"You've been avoiding me, right? Let me tell you something. This morning I heard Ratface tell Slinger and Moaner that he's staying here permanently from now on. He wants to take over Stefan's education and he wants to make this place the League's headquarters. Ratface is no joke, you know, and he's getting worse. So, tell me, Max— does that change things?"

Max nodded dumbly. It did.

"So, how are we going to get out of here?" she demanded. "Or haven't you been thinking about it?"

Stung by her tone, Max tried to concentrate. "We could put a ladder against the fence."

"Too clumsy," Christina said. "And we might touch the top wire."

"What if we threw a tarp over the top wire?"

"No. Too heavy, too clumsy to carry. Plus we wouldn't have time to fetch all our gear, *and* Stefan, *and* a ladder, *and* a tarp. This has to be quick and clean."

Max had been thinking about electricity. Suddenly he knew how they'd do it. He grinned. "We'll go through the gate," he said.

"How?"

"Switch off the electricity."

She was about to say something critical, but stopped and said thoughtfully, "How?"

"The master switch. It's in the fuse box on the wall by the back door."

"Moron—the box is locked."

"So we'll find the key. When the time comes, we'll sneak out and unlock the fuse box and turn off the master switch. With the power off we'll be able to slide open the catch on the gate without electrocuting ourselves."

"Good. We'll do it tonight."

Max felt himself grow tense with fear. "Tonight? You're nuts. Ratface is here."

"He's here to stay, Max," Christina said patiently. "We've got no choice."

"But he'll come after us."

"We'll have a head start," Christina said. "Come on, are you with me or not?"

Max sighed. "I'm with you. Tonight it is."

At that moment, Ratface looked across at them from the perimeter fence. It was a slit-eyed stare that seemed to say, I know what you're thinking.

10

RATFACE crossed the yard until he stood in front of them. He stared first at Max and then at Christina. When he spoke finally, his voice was mild. "What were you talking about?"

Christina looked up at his face in fascination. She tried to imagine that she didn't know him and was meeting him for the first time. He was sharp, slender, and quick, as if constructed entirely of nerve endings. There was no clear expression on his face, but his eyes were bright and searching. He would break her if he could. Right now she could feel him probing her heart, her mind, finding her hopes and fears, her strengths and weaknesses. She trembled, looked away. "Nothing," she muttered.

"Nothing?" said Ratface. "I wish I had the time

to talk about nothing. I wish I could simply please myself." He sat between them on the edge of the veranda. "But I can't. Do you know why?"

Christina hated it when Ratface was like this. She was silent, knowing he would soon answer his own question.

"Because I've got responsibilities," Ratface said. "You two can sit in the sun, but I have the needs of the League to consider."

Christina felt his hand like a manacle on her forearm. He bent his head until she could feel his breath on the side of her face. His words were slow, deliberate: "The League must not be allowed to decline."

Christina tried to jerk her arm away, but his grip tightened and he showed his teeth at her in his version of a smile. "In isolation we grow in purity and strength."

He seemed to emit a cold draft of madness, aiming it at her like a weapon. She closed her eyes, thinking, *I will not listen.* She hoped, guiltily, that he would release her and focus his attention on Max.

And then, under the odor of his glittering obsessions, she caught a gust of peppermint and perspiration. He's flesh and blood, just like me, she thought. He's dangerous, but there's nothing special about him. I can beat him. She turned, stared, as he went on with his White League nonsense: "Soon we will bring a white light into the darkness."

Gawd, what a joke. Christina eased out of his

grasp. If you want to lighten the darkness, how about buying a brighter light for my bedroom?

She didn't say it aloud. She could say things like that only to Max. She looked out across the compound to the surrounding mountains. Storm clouds were gathering, blotting out the winter sun. In the yard, Slinger and Moaner continued to walk with Stefan. They kept glancing at Ratface. They're nervous, she thought. They know we're unhappy. They know Stefan is homesick. They've got doubts about Ratface.

At that moment, Ratface seemed to read her thoughts. She tried not to let it unsettle her. He said, pointing across the yard at Stefan, "Children are our hope. One day you will have families of your own, and teach them to be custodians of the work of the League for *their* children. I can think of no better way to express love."

Some love, Christina thought. Real love isn't fearful and narrow and ignorant. Real love doesn't say that some people are better than others.

Ratface went on: "You two are lucky. So is Arne. I found him before he could be corrupted. He was a neglected child, roaming the streets. He lacked guidance. I have saved him."

Without thinking, Christina exploded. "How many others have you kidnapped?"

She felt Ratface stiffen—but he didn't rebuke her; he just said gently, "No others. And I didn't steal him, I saved him."

He looked piercingly at her. She felt the force of his personality and looked away, wrapping her arms about herself for comfort. He was sitting too close to her and she couldn't bear it.

Then he stood up. He laughed abruptly, hollowly. "Enough of this sitting around." He looked at them quizzically. "If I were a suspicious man I'd think you two were plotting something."

"Us?" Christina said. "What would we be plotting?"

Ratface didn't reply. They watched him cross the yard and join the others.

"Well?" Christina said. "Are you still game?"

Max stared coldly at her. "Give me some credit, Christina."

It was her turn to blush. "Sorry, Max."

"I'm going to look for the fuse box key."

"I'll help you."

They entered the house together. They had about five minutes, Christina thought, before the adults grew suspicious and came in after them.

They started with the kitchen, searching quickly through all the drawers. They found plenty of old door and car keys, and a couple of rusted padlocks, but no keys that would suit the small, shiny new lock on the fuse box.

"Where now?"

"The pantry," Max said.

Christina had always disliked the pantry. It smelled stale. The shelves groaned beneath the weight of thick jars, biscuit tins, and cardboard boxes. Sacks of flour and sugar were stacked on the floor, and a narrow broom closet had been built into the back wall. They went to work.

They didn't notice that Moaner had entered the house. They didn't know that she was standing outside the pantry, watching them. "Lost something?" she asked.

Max crammed the lid back on the box of shoe polish and brushes. He turned to look at Moaner. He'll reveal everything, Christina thought, knowing how he always wilted under pressure.

But this time he surprised her. Looking levelly at Moaner, he said, "We're searching for a button to sew on Harvey Two. He's missing an eye."

There was a long pause. Finally Moaner said, "My sewing basket's in the sitting room. Try looking there."

Then she turned to Christina. "I don't keep buttons in the broom closet, Olwen."

Christina shut the closet door. She gave Moaner a wide, innocent smile. No, she wanted to reply— but you do hide keys there, on hooks behind the brooms.

11

MAX SAT UP in bed, listening intently.

Nothing. The house was silent. Time to get ready.

First he tiptoed across the room to the door and opened it a crack. He wanted plenty of warning if one of the adults was out there roaming around the house. He waited for a moment, listening, reassuring himself that it was safe, then crossed to his bed to start packing.

He opened a drawer and put the lighted candle in it. It gave enough light to dress by, but not enough to penetrate the blackness of the corridor. Then, shivering in the cold air, he dressed rapidly in warm underclothes, a thick shirt, a wool sweater, thick work trousers, and two pairs of socks. He sat down on the bed to tie the laces of his hiking boots. The rubber soles always squeaked, but that couldn't be helped. His ordinary work boots, with their nailed leather soles, would have sounded like a herd of elephants in the darkness. Finally he strapped on his watch. Half past twelve. He hoped Christina had stayed awake.

Hanging on the back of the door was his winter jacket. It was wind- and waterproof, with large pockets and a hood. During the day he had made several trips to his room, each time with a different item for their escape. In one pocket were the flashlight and a plastic bottle of water, and in another the matches, candles, paper bags, and a tin opener. At the last minute he had decided to add a handful of Band-Aids out of the medicine cabinet and taken the key to the fuse box.

He was relying on Christina to bring the food, her knife, and another water bottle, but where was she? He sat and waited, thinking through their plan. Quarter to one.

His head whirled with questions. Should I go and see if she's awake? Does she need help? Should I start to get Stefan ready?

He decided that it was too risky to go to her room. The less walking up and down the better. All the bedrooms were along the corridor. More than anything, he didn't want to wake Ratface.

He opened a drawer and took out clothes for Stefan. He put a couple of handkerchiefs in a pocket, knowing that he would need them for Stefan. Just then the floor squeaked. He held his breath.

"Max? Are you awake?"

Christina slipped into the room as she spoke. "Sorry I took so long," she whispered.

"Where were you? It's nearly one o'clock. We have to go."

"I couldn't steal enough food during the day, so I was in the pantry."

Max looked at her bulging pockets. "What did you get?"

"Bread, cheese, apples, and some nuts and raisins."

He nodded. "Good. Now let's dress Stefan and get out of here."

"Okay."

Christina sat on the edge of Stefan's bed and gently stroked his chest. "Stef," she whispered. "Stef—time to wake up."

Stefan stirred, coughed weakly, and rolled over. Suddenly he sat up and opened his mouth to yell. Christina immediately put her hand over his mouth, held him against her body, and rocked him in her arms. "Shh," she crooned. "It's all right. We're taking you home. Would you like that?"

She removed her hand. Stefan spoke his first words in two weeks. "Home?" he said loudly. "Are we going home?"

"Shh," she said. "Yes, home to your mother, but you have to be very quiet. Promise?"

Stefan nodded and scrambled out of bed. Already he looked much happier. He grabbed Harvey Two and started to run toward the door.

Max caught him. "Put some warm clothes on first," he said. "And be quiet."

Stefan went still and wary, as if he had remembered something. "I want my real mother."

"That's where we're going," Max said. "That's why you can't wake up the others."

Apparently satisfied, Stefan let himself be dressed in Max's old clothes. Now and then he sniffed and coughed.

"He'll need a coat," Max said. "We can't take him outside without a coat. It's cold and damp out there."

"I'll be all right," Stefan said.

Max smiled at him. "Will you? No, we'd better find you something warm to wear."

He gave Christina the flashlight, picked up Stefan and Harvey Two, and led the way into the corridor. They stepped softly past the other bedrooms, and then into the kitchen. They were moving by instinct through the dark house, but once or twice Christina flicked the flashlight on and off to check for obstacles. Finally they were on the veranda. Max put Stefan down and said, "What can we do about getting him a coat?"

Christina was rummaging in the old wardrobe by the back door. "There's this," she said, holding up a yellow slicker belonging to Moaner. "We could shorten it."

She cut the slicker to size, fitted it over Stefan's shoulders, and pulled the hood over his head. Finally she tied string around his waist like a belt. "Perfect fit!" she whispered.

Stefan grinned. Max was doubtful. Stefan looked very odd, like a bright, top-heavy scarecrow swamped by meters of bright yellow material.

"Ready?" he asked impatiently.

"Ready."

"Then let's go."

The air was cold; the wind sounded lonely in the pine trees. An animal brushed through the under-growth. There was no moon, only the blackness of thick clouds above. That was no help. Max hoped the flashlight batteries would last.

Christina held the flashlight while he stood on the crate of firewood and reached up to the fuse box on the wall next to the door. Max had never seen inside it, but Slinger had once explained it to him, warning him never to touch it.

He slid the little key into the padlock, turned it, removed the padlock. He opened the door of the box. There was not enough light to see by. "Give me the light," he said.

Christina handed him the flashlight and he shone the beam on the dials, switches, and fuses deep within the box. The master switch was in the down position. Holding the flashlight with one hand, he reached in with the other. A few centimeters short. He stood on tiptoe and reached again.

The crate rocked a little under his toes.

He stretched again. His fingers touched the switch.

Then, in a frightening instant, he felt the crate slide out from under him. Even as his fingers flicked the switch upward, he was falling.

The crate toppled over, smashing onto its side. Firewood spilled out, rolling and thumping across the veranda like noises out of a nightmare.

Max landed painfully, his knees knocking against the edge of the crate. He felt dazed and winded. He didn't know if he could walk. But he did know that he had made enough noise to wake a whole town.

But somehow he had saved the flashlight, hugging it against his chest. He thrust it at Christina. "Run!" he whispered urgently. "Run!"

Christina, dragging Stefan by the hand, disappeared into the darkness. Max got awkwardly to his feet. He began to shuffle after her, following the jerky glow from the flashlight. He heard her slide back the bolt on the gate, saw her push it open. There was a flash of light on Stefan's yellow hood.

Then he saw that they were free. Their feet pounded down the track beyond the electric fence.

He tried to hurry. He sensed, without turning around, that the long, curving fingers of Ratface were reaching through the dark.

Then he felt them.

12

AT SIX O'CLOCK the next morning, Max shivered awake, holding his arms around his chest. He had slept fitfully, tormented by discomfort and the chilly concrete floor he'd been forced to sleep on.

Ratface had thrown him into the generator shed. It was a small building constructed of corrugated iron sheets bolted to a metal frame. A large diesel engine took up most of the space. The batteries were on a bench at the back of the shed. Tins of fuel were stored under another bench at the side of the shed. Spare coils of wire hung from hooks on the walls, and dusty insulators were heaped in a cardboard box. Otherwise the building was empty.

Max groaned. He got to his feet and did stretching exercises to get warm and ease his knotted muscles. For the moment, he didn't feel able to concentrate on anything else. He knew that if he started thinking about Christina, about being separated from her, maybe forever, he would collapse inside.

He also knew that he had changed in a way that he would find difficult to describe to anyone. In defying Ratface—and the White League—he felt that he had crossed an invisible line.

But, at the same time, he felt a twinge of guilt for wanting to abandon Slinger and Moaner. He tried to forget that. He tried to concentrate on his stiff, cramped limbs, not on his thoughts or feelings.

Thirty minutes later, he heard voices in the yard. Then the electric gate opened and he heard a car drive away. They've gone to look for Christina and Stefan, he thought.

At nine o'clock the shed door was unlocked. Slinger, eyes averted, silently handed him a tray of food. Moaner must have gone with Ratface, he thought.

Then Slinger started the diesel generator and left, locking the door again. Time passed. It was torture. The engine noise was stupefying in that enclosed space. Max put his hands over his ears. He could scarcely think straight. He looked dismally at the tray on the cold concrete floor. Breakfast: a glass of water and a slice of bread.

An hour later, the car came back. This time

Ratface unlocked the door and indicated that Max should follow him. They crossed the yard to the house and entered the kitchen. Ratface pointed silently at a chair, waited until Max was seated, then sat opposite him.

He said nothing. There was no sign of Slinger or Moaner.

The minutes ticked by. Finally Max couldn't stand it. He stood up, shouting, "What have you done with the others?"

Ratface immediately took him back to the shed and locked the door. But Max felt relief. Christina and Stefan got away, he thought. Ratface hasn't been able to find them.

At eleven o'clock he was fetched again, this time by Slinger. Again he was taken to the kitchen. Ratface and Moaner were there. Ratface pushed Max onto a chair and kept his hands on Max's shoulders restrainingly.

Ratface started.

"Where are they?"

"Who?" said Max.

Ratface's fingers tightened.

"I'll ask just once more. Where are Olwen and Arne?"

"I don't know."

"Where were you going?"

"Taking Stefan home."

"Who?"

"Stefan! Stefan! Stefan!" Max shouted.

"Don't, Kenelm," said Moaner anxiously. "This is Arne's home."

"We were taking him to his *real* home," Max said.

Ratface bent his face down to Max's ear and asked softly, "How were you going to get there? What direction were you going to take? How were you going to travel?"

Max said, "We weren't afraid. We would have made it. I bet Christina and Stefan are already there."

He fervently hoped that Christina would keep going without him. He wished for her success, even though life would be unbearable without her.

"They're lost," Ratface said. "They're cold, afraid, hungry, desperate. We are going out there again to find them. They will be so miserable they will run into our arms."

The voice was slow, mesmerizing. Max fought against the power of it. "You'll never find them," he stammered. "Christina's clever, cleverer than you, cleverer than Mother or Father."

Ratface tapped his knuckles on Max's skull. "Arne has a bad cold," he said. "He'll get worse. Olwen will not be able to look after him. She'll be forced to bring him back."

Max would not let himself be persuaded. "They've got food and warm clothes," he said.

In his treacherous, dreamy voice, Ratface said, "I wonder where they spent the night? I can just imagine it, the pair of them sitting on the damp ground under a tree. The cold wind blowing. Arne coughing miserably, crying ceaselessly, Olwen powerless to help him. Can't you just picture their misery, Mother?"

Anxiously wringing her hands, Moaner begged, "Please tell us, Kenelm."

Ratface said, "They don't have a chance. In fact, Kenelm is lucky he's safe and warm and dry here with us. He's probably so relieved he doesn't care about Olwen and Arne anymore."

Slinger said, "There's only one logical route they could have taken. With three of us looking, we'll find them in no time."

"I wonder what they'll say to Kenelm when they see him again?" said Ratface, his fingers tightening again on Max's shoulders. He leaned down close to Max's ear. "They won't want anything to do with you. They'll think you're a coward who gave up, or they'll hate you for not sending us to save them sooner."

Max stiffened in the chair. *I will not listen. I will not believe you.* He tried to tell himself that Ratface was afraid.

But Ratface didn't seem afraid. And he was giving courage to Slinger and Moaner.

"I'm locking you up again now," said Ratface. "I don't think you'll get into any more mischief."

Max was taken back to the generator shed. He peered out through a gap near the door. A little later he saw the car being backed out and driven up to the electric gate. Moaner got out and approached the shed. She unlocked the door and handed him apples, carrots, raisins, and a slice of dry bread.

"Don't worry, dear," she said, avoiding his eyes. "I hope we won't be long."

Max opened his mouth to speak. If he had Christina's skills and forcefulness, he'd work on Moaner, take advantage of her essential kindness.

Too late. She went out, locking the door behind her. Max peered through the gap again. He saw the gate slide open, the car leave, the gate slam shut. He slumped miserably against the wall.

13

HUNGER PANGS roused him. Max found an empty sack, sat on it, and began to eat an apple.

There seemed to be no way out of the shed. It would be no good to run an electric current to the door to electrocute Ratface, Slinger, or Moaner, because he would still be on the inside. He couldn't think of any way to use the diesel fuel. Without a shovel he couldn't dig a tunnel, even if he could break through the concrete floor. He didn't even have the matches or the tin opener any longer. They had been confiscated by Ratface, along with the candles and water bottle.

He got up and examined the bolts that held the corrugated iron walls to the metal frame. Perhaps if he undid enough of them he could push aside a flap of iron. He emptied boxes and looked on shelves and under the bench, but there were no tools. He tried to undo the nuts with his fingers, but succeeded only in tearing his fingernails. The noise of the engine was confusing him. He switched it off, sat on the sack again, and tried to think clearly.

Engine, fuel, batteries, boxes of dusty odds and ends. Nothing to help him there.

Bits and pieces of electrical cable, bottles of chemicals, spare fan belts for the generator.

Wait a minute. What was in the bottles?

Max hurried across to the shelf and brushed the dust off the labels. Turpentine was in the first bottle, linseed oil in the second, and battery acid in the third. I might be able to use the acid for something, he thought.

He looked wildly around the shed. The padlock and latch were on the outside of the door, so that was no help. There wasn't enough acid to burn a hole in anything, let alone the wall.

He thought again about the corrugated iron that formed the walls of the shed, about the nuts and bolts holding the sheets to the frame, about the rust that made the nuts immovable.

Using a shred of burlap from the sack he had been sitting on, Max brushed a little of the acid onto a rusty nut. After a while there was a faint hissing and evidence of the rust loosening. He tapped the nut with a small piece of iron. It moved stiffly at first, but, eventually, by protecting his fingers with his handkerchief, he was able to undo it.

Working quickly, he chose one sheet of iron and coated the nine nuts and bolts with the battery acid. They seemed to take forever to loosen. He was forced to chip away at two of the nuts. A third would not loosen because the bolt was bent. Every few seconds he stopped to listen for the car, and he came close to panicking as he fumbled and spilled acid onto his sweater sleeve.

Forty-five minutes passed before he was able to remove all but the nut with the bent bolt. He put the remaining food in his pockets, stepped up to the sheet of iron, and kicked it firmly several times. Some of the bolts screeched as they came free of their holes, but now he could see the light outside. He gave one final, heavy kick, and the iron sheet swung free of the wall, bending where the last bolt still held it.

He was free. The time was two o'clock in the afternoon, and Christina and Stefan were more than twelve hours ahead of him.

Free, but not free. One fearful touch of the fence told him that it was electrified. The charge punched along his arm and left him feeling dazed and tingling for several seconds. When he recovered he ran to the garden shed, grabbed a crowbar, and dragged it to the veranda. There was a shiny new lock on the fuse box. In a fury he smashed the crowbar at it until the buckled door swung open and he could turn off the master switch.

Should he look for the equipment Ratface had taken from him?

Should he grab more food from the kitchen? After all, he hadn't had much to eat today.

No. He'd wasted too much time already. And they might come back at any minute.

He ran.

14

THE NIGHT BEFORE, when Max had fallen, Christina had been paralyzed with fear. She had been eagerly watching him one moment, and then overwhelmed by the terrible noise the next. It had taken her a few seconds to register that Max was telling her to run.

All her actions after that were panicky and instinctive. She grabbed Stefan's hand and dashed with him to the gate, not knowing if Max was following her or not. She didn't stop. At the gate she grasped the latch, expecting it would be locked, fearing an electric charge would burn her arm.

But the heavy gate swung free. She hauled Stefan through the gap and they stumbled down the road. After a while she switched off the flashlight, feeling too exposed with it on. Suddenly the night was very black, very close. She veered off the road and into the forest. She thought she heard a shout behind her, but all she wanted to do was get as far away as possible. Small branches slapped at her face. Something scratched her cheek. Stefan fell over twice, and he was sobbing noisily. But she didn't dare use the flashlight.

And she didn't dare stop. She half carried, half dragged Stefan further into the forest. Now that Ratface, Slinger, and Moaner were alerted, it would be pointless to hide near the road. She must find a warm, dry spot where they could rest and she could plan what to do next. Everything was up to her now. She might never see Max again. She assumed that he had been captured, but she couldn't risk going back to find him. The whole thing was a disaster. She was sobbing from exhaustion, fear, and loneliness.

She didn't know what time it was or how long they'd been crashing through the forest. Her movements became slow, automatic, so that when she collided with a wall of some kind, she was not badly hurt. She sank to her knees, put one arm around Stefan, and touched the wall with her free hand.

It had the warped, splintery texture of old boards. Still holding Stefan, she trailed her knuckles against the wall and began to explore the structure. Apparently it was a small hut, perhaps a shelter for hunters or lumbermen. There was a bolt but no lock on the door.

She debated with herself briefly and then decided: This will have to do. We can't go any farther tonight. We'll take the risk.

She drew the bolt out and pushed open the door. It swung easily and silently on its hinges. The air smelled stale and dusty.

Finally she risked using the flashlight. The burst of light startled her after the utter darkness of the forest. She saw a dirt floor, a mattress on an iron frame, a small wooden table with one chair, and, in a corner, a moldy, warped cardboard suitcase. On a shelf near the bed were two candle stubs, an enamel mug, and a tin of baked beans. Old beer bottles and newspapers had been dumped in another corner. Neither the candles nor the baked beans were of much use to her—Max had the matches and the tin opener.

"Yuck," said Stefan. He sniffed; soon his teeth began to chatter.

Christina knelt and held his face between her hands. "We'll be warm and cozy here," she said. "We'll go to bed now and leave in the morning."

"I want to go home," said Stefan. "I don't want to stay here." He began to cry.

Oh, hell, thought Christina. Don't do that. We haven't got Max to help us. I can't manage if you fall in a heap now. Aloud she said, "It's too far, Stef. We don't want to get lost in the dark, do we? We'll find your mum in the morning."

She brushed dust off the mattress and lay on her side, hugging Stefan's small, cold, bony back while he hugged Harvey Two. There were no blankets or pillows. The mattress was lumpy and unpleasant. Stefan fell asleep quickly, but Christina lay awake for a long time, trying to think clearly, trying to plan for the morning. When that didn't work, she tried to will herself to fall asleep, but stupid thoughts, colors, conversations, and snatches of the Leader's boring lectures kept crowding her mind.

Eventually she fell asleep. She dreamed that she was rowing again. The island, the waving figure, seemed to mock her, and she woke to the sound of Stefan coughing. He had fallen out of bed and was lying half-asleep on the chilly floor, his knees drawn up to his chest. The weak light of dawn was showing around the door frame of the windowless hut.

Christina lifted Stefan onto the bed and draped her coat over him. She felt sad and useless. Who was she kidding? She'd never manage this alone. Only partially awake, she began to search for the water bottle.

It was missing. She must have dropped it the night before. Fighting disappointment, she did stretching exercises to help herself wake up. After a few minutes, her spirits improved. She filled her palm with nuts and raisins and began to eat.

Suddenly she stopped, opened the packet, and poured the nuts and raisins back in. I must think clearly, she told herself. Nuts and raisins are light, easy to carry, and nourishing. I should eat something bulkier, to lighten the load.

But she had only cheese, apples, and bread.

And the tin of baked beans. She took the tin down from the shelf and turned it around in her hands. The thought of eating cold baked beans in the morning—or at any time—made her feel queasy. But baked beans would be very filling for both of them—if she could get Stefan to eat any. And if she could get the tin open.

When all else fails, use force, she told herself finally. She opened a narrow, pointed gadget on her pocketknife, looked around for a stone to use as a hammer, and began to punch holes in the lid of the tin.

Soon it was a gaping, jagged mess. The strong-smelling juice splashed on her hands. But the opening was large enough.

Spitting on her handkerchief, she wiped dust from the inside of the mug and shook the beans into it. They glugged and slurped. She wrinkled her nose. Yuckeroo. Then, tipping the cup, and using a hunk of the bread, she managed to swallow half of the contents of the tin. She burped. Is this what it's like for homeless people? she wondered.

Time to wake Stefan. She shook his shoulder gently. "Stef. Wake up."

The little boy seemed dazed. He was shivering. Christina held her hand to his forehead. She thought his temperature had risen during the night, but she wasn't sure. "Stef," she said. "Uppety-up. Time for breakfast."

Getting Stefan to eat the remainder of the baked beans was almost impossible. He complained—*Yuck!*—closed his mouth, shook his head. To distract him she told him stories and jokes, made the coming day sound like an adventure, and asked him to imagine being home again. Gradually his spirits lifted. He finished the beans almost without being aware of them.

Christina checked her watch. Six-thirty. Time to take stock of her surroundings. She put her hand on Stefan's shoulder. "I want you to stay here, Stef, while I check outside. I won't be long."

"No! Don't leave me!"

"I won't be far away. Just outside."

"Don't leave me!"

Christina sighed. "All right. Come on. Are you warm enough?"

His teeth were chattering. He looked feverish, but Christina realized that she, too, felt very cold. The little hut offered no warmth.

Hang on. Newspapers. A stack of them lay in a corner of the hut. The bottom ones would be damp, but not the top ones. Newspaper insulates, Christina told herself, and you can light fires with it.

She also remembered something they'd forgotten to bring with them. Making a game of it, she and Stefan began to tear a couple of sheets into small squares to use as toilet paper.

Then they quickly stripped off the outer layers of their clothing, wrapped themselves in newspaper, and dressed again. "It's working," Christina said. "I feel warmer already. Do you, Stef?"

His pale face was uncertain. "I think so."

I'll have to jolly him the whole way, she thought. Everything will have to be turned into a game or he'll just give up.

She smiled at him and began to march around the room. "Listen," she said. Her newspaper underclothes were rustling like dry leaves. "Rustle, rustle, crush, crush."

Stefan began to smile. He joined her in their manic stamp around the rickety table, shouting, "Rustle, rustle, crush, crush!"

"Okay," Christina said, "now let's go and see where we are."

15

SHE LOADED HER POCKETS with all their possessions and they stepped outside. The dawn fog was lifting and she saw at once that the hut stood at the base of a tall wooden structure topped with a glass-enclosed cabin. A sign on it read DISTRICT FIRE AUTHORITY.

"What's that?" Stefan said.

"It's used for spotting forest fires."

Stefan looked around in alarm. "Where?"

"Don't worry, Stef," Christina said. "It's too wet for fires."

She looked about her at the dense, looming trees. The air was damp and chilly. The forest seemed to blanket all sounds except for the scratches and tumbles of birds grubbing among the fallen leaves.

Not quite. She stiffened, alerted by the low growl of a slow-moving vehicle somewhere to the left of them. Ratface. She was sure of it. Now that it was daylight he would be out looking for them. She tried to anticipate how he'd go about it. She didn't think he'd search the area near the compound yet. He'd assume they would have gone as far as possible down the road.

She waited, listening, as the engine noise receded into the distance, then continued her investigation. The hut and tower stood in a clearing. Some empty drums and coiled hoses lay on the ground nearby. The only other feature of interest was a rough dirt road through the forest. It was dead straight and seemed to cut to the edge of the world, scarring every peak in the mountain range. It was clearly unused. She guessed that fire fighters used it as an access road.

She kept thinking about the tower. She would be able to see everything from up there.

She leaned down and put her hands on Stefan's shoulders. "Wouldn't it be fun to climb to the top of the tower?"

He nodded doubtfully.

"Okay, then. Let's try it," she said.

Five minutes later she was forced to give up. Stefan soon grew weak and unresponsive. They were only two meters off the ground when he started to shake, his eyes tightly closed.

"All right, Stef, down we go."

At the bottom again he moaned and sat on the

ground, coughing. He needs warmth and rest, Christina thought.

"Stef," she said, "I want you to rest for a few minutes. I'm going to climb the tower and see where we are. Okay?"

He didn't have the energy to complain. She put him on the filthy mattress in the hut and sat with him for a while, stroking his cheek. His breathing grew less forced. When he was asleep she returned to the tower.

A few minutes later, crouching so that she couldn't be seen, Christina was looking out onto a great expanse of forest. Here and there, dirt roads scribbled across it. Smudges of distant mountains defined the horizon. Otherwise there were only colored specks that must be the rooftops of the farm buildings she knew so well.

It occurred to her then that she knew the tower after all. She'd been glimpsing a corner of it from Slinger's woodpile all these years but had taken it for granted.

Dense, waving treetops obscured her view, but she was able to see most of the compound. She watched for several minutes. Just when she had decided it was deserted, she saw a tiny figure leave the house and cross to the generator shed. A moment later, the figure returned to the house.

Slinger? It looked like him.

But where were the others? Out searching? She circled the observation platform, peering through the trees. Unfortunately she could see only a short stretch of the road. She checked the time: nine o'clock.

She had two options: watch the compound until she knew whether Max had been captured, or walk cross-country to freedom. Both options had disadvantages. If she waited, she'd lose valuable time, and Ratface might find her. If she set out with Stefan, she might never know Max's fate. Worst of all, she'd be in the world alone. Max could be too cautious sometimes, too dutiful and respectful, but they gave each other strength. Together, they might succeed. Separate, they could easily fail.

She decided to wait. It was warm behind the glass, now that the sun was rising. From time to time she checked on Stefan by looking down at the hut or listening from the top of the steps. She saw and heard nothing. He'll sleep for a while, she thought, and call to me when he wakes up.

Poor Stefan. She imagined his fear the day Ratface picked him up: the long drive into the hills, the soft, cruel voice saying, "Your mother didn't want you." Ratface had said that Stefan was neglected. How would he know? Had he been watching, assessing, waiting to swoop down on Stefan and carry him away? And what gave him the right to decide who was neglected and who wasn't?

She shivered.

She tried to see it from the point of view of Slinger and Moaner. She was certain they were having doubts about Ratface. But they were too cut off from the outside world and too intimidated to investigate what Ratface was up to.

Suddenly, Christina was haunted by the lonely figure in her dream. Was her mother alive? Or was Christina truly alone in the world? She felt uprooted, as if she belonged nowhere and might blow away and be forgotten.

Then something moved in the compound. She ducked. Peering above the rail, she saw Ratface park the car, get out, and walk to the generator shed.

A moment later, her spirits surged. Max was still in the compound.

She watched Ratface take Max across to the house, and she waited, curious. A moment later, they returned to the generator shed, and Ratface went back to the house alone.

What was going on?

Again she waited. Half an hour later, when nothing else had happened, she began to feel restless. The newspaper undergarments were making her perspire. She shrugged her shoulders and tugged at her clothes, trying to get more comfortable.

At eleven o'clock she saw Slinger cross the yard, unlock the generator shed, and take Max back to the house. They were in there for thirty minutes this time, and then Max was locked up again.

Soon after that the three adults drove away from the compound. Christina thought: This is it, my only chance to release him.

She ran to the steps and almost flung herself down them. It's not going to be easy, she thought. Stefan will be a burden, and I don't know how I'll unlock the shed door.

She reached the bottom of the tower and ran to the door of the hut. "Stef," she called. "Wake up. Time to . . ."

Her voice trailed away. The hut was empty.

16

HER SKIN WENT COLD. Her throat tightened. Her heart hammered. She wanted to collapse onto the ground. She made herself take deep breaths. *Control yourself. He can't be far away.*

She stepped into the clearing and curved her hands next to her mouth. Turning to project her voice in all directions, knowing she risked being heard in the compound, she shouted, "Stefan! Stefan!"

She listened. No answer. Panic rose in her again. *He was my responsibility and I let him wander away.*

She forced herself to imagine how a sick, frightened seven-year-old might think. Given that the whole forest looked forbidding, which part would he find least scary? Ahead of her was the fire-access road. All else was a solid barrier of trees.

100

The road, she thought.

She set off at a steady run. *He's so small. Small and weak. He could easily die.*

The road had a bone-jarring surface treacherous with puddles, ditches, and stones. Twice she fell, slamming hard onto the ground. She called Stefan's name until she was hoarse.

After ten minutes, she slowed to think. How long had she been in the tower? Almost two hours. Stefan had slept, but for how long? Did he walk, or run? How much ground could he have covered?

I'm just wasting time, she thought. I can't do this alone. He probably hasn't even come this way. And if I start searching the forest, I'll waste more time. I must free Max first. Then we'll work it out together.

She returned to the tower, judged the direction in which the compound lay, and entered the forest.

It was not so frightening in daylight. Grass and fallen leaves were soft under her feet. The air carried the comforting scent of resin. She was able to dodge the low, whipping branches and managed to push through the trees at a steady jog.

A few minutes later, the forest's gloom softened. Then she was at the edge of the trees, looking out at the dirt road and the compound gate at the end of it.

Before venturing out of the trees, she automatically glanced back down the road—and froze. There, parked at the side of the road in the distance, was Ratface's car. She jerked back her head, then looked again. As far as she could tell, the car was empty.

But she guessed what they might be doing. Either they had seen Stefan and stopped for him, or they had decided to search the hut and the tower.

No time to spare. Christina stepped onto the dirt road and ran hard toward the compound.

It wasn't until she reached the gate that she realized she didn't know how she would get into the compound itself. Frustrated, she kicked the gate.

It moved.

She stepped back, expecting a trap, expecting an alarm to ring. When nothing happened, she extended her foot and pushed. The gate swung open.

How careless, she thought. She slipped through the gap and ran toward the generator shed.

"Max," she whispered, tapping urgently on the door. "Max."

No answer. Maybe they had hurt him. Maybe he was unconscious. She rattled the door. Firmly locked.

Puzzled now, she started to investigate. At the back of the shed, obscured by empty fuel drums, she came upon a hole in the wall and a loose flap of iron.

He was gone.

What now? She was glad he'd escaped, but now she would have to find him again. And Stefan. Did this mean a return to the forest? She groaned at the prospect. Should she keep searching, or try to make it alone?

Christina left the compound and began to walk parallel to the road, keeping a few meters back among the trees. She would not risk heading cross-country through the forest. She might get lost and never be found. Surely the road led somewhere, perhaps to a way out of the mountains and down to the city.

As she drew near Ratface's car, she slowed her pace, alert for the sound of the adults returning through the trees. When she was opposite the driver's door, she stopped, looked about her, and darted across to the car. It took her only a second to check the ignition. No key.

Oh well, she couldn't drive anyway, so it was no great disappointment. She set off again.

For the next twenty minutes, Christina stumbled over fallen logs and brushed aside saplings and tree ferns as the dirt road dipped and curved through the forest. Her footsteps became plodding and automatic, her mind blank.

And so it took her a moment to register that a small figure was walking dejectedly in the center of the road ahead of her, and that a car was on the road somewhere behind her, the sound faint and distant but getting closer.

She stopped, paralyzed with indecision. She was too far away to warn Stefan. The car—she was sure it was Ratface's—was only seconds away. When it rounded the bend, Ratface would spot Stefan immediately. Stefan hadn't the sense or the energy to duck among the trees. His head was down. Harvey

Two dangled from his right hand. His feet were dragging as though he would welcome being found by Ratface.

Then three things happened together. Ratface's car slowed for the bend in the road, Christina ducked among the bushes, and a gray shape darted onto the road and scooped Stefan to safety.

17

"CALM DOWN, Stef, Max said softly. "It's me. Max."

The little body stopped squirming. Max took his hand away from Stefan's mouth, turned him around, and smiled. "It's only me. Are you all right? Where's Christina?"

They were crouched behind a clump of spindly trees at the edge of the road. In the distance, Ratface's car rounded another bend and disappeared. Max touched the boy's tear-streaked cheeks. "Stef? Where's Christina?"

No reply. Then Stefan's eyes brightened and he pointed over Max's shoulder. Max turned and peered between the screening branches. His heart lifted. Christina was running down the road toward them, smiling.

He stood up. "Hey! Here. Quick."

He'd never felt so warmed by a smile. She veered off the road, plunged through branches and leaves, and hugged him tight against her, knocking the breath from his body.

She began laughing and talking at once, giving him smacking kisses and wrapping him in her arms. Then she released him and knelt to kiss and hug Stefan. "I thought I'd lost you both. I thought it was all over. Now we can start again."

Max watched her. Then he grew irritated with her. The prowling car might return at any moment, they were still in danger, yet Christina seemed to be bubbling over as if they hadn't a worry in the world. He looked at his watch. "We have to think," he said urgently. "We're hours behind schedule and we've lost our head start."

Christina stood up. She couldn't figure him out. Wasn't he glad to see her? She touched his arm. "At least we've escaped. At least we're together."

He frowned. "All I'm saying is, we can't just blunder on without a plan."

"I know that."

"Do you? I don't think you realize that we've still got a long way to go, we've lost some of our supplies, and we might have to carry Stefan."

"I know," Christina said again.

What's gotten into him? she thought. Here we are, halfway to freedom, and he's arguing with me.

"Our situation is twice as bad as it was," Max said, "and we have to be twice as careful."

Christina was annoyed. "We'll manage, Max. Don't get all stuffy on me."

But Max couldn't help himself. He had been badly frightened in the last few hours. Now, in his relief at finding Christina and Stefan again, he wanted to gain control so there'd be no more mistakes. He drew himself up, bristling at her.

"*Manage?* Didn't manage Stefan too well, did you? He spent all night alone in the forest, I suppose."

Christina slapped him hard. "Enough! He wandered off only an hour ago, while I was planning how to set you free."

Max jerked away, shocked and hurt. But his tension begin to ease. "I'm sorry. I feel all . . ."

He couldn't finish, couldn't explain himself. Christina continued to glare at him. Then, just as he turned miserably away, she relented. "It's okay. I understand. I'm all upside-down, too. Part of me feels bad for running away, part of me feels scared, and part of me feels we're doing the right thing."

Max smiled in relief. Her feelings were like his own.

"But mostly," Christina went on, "I think we should just concentrate on getting away from here. It'll be dark soon, and we have to find shelter."

"But we can't just head off in any old direction."

Christina said patiently, "I was up in the tower this morning. I saw a fire-access road. That will lead us to a town or a main road. And it will be easier to travel on than bashing through the forest."

Max pretended to think about it. In fact, he knew that they had no alternative. Not only had she surveyed the area, she had also survived a night away from the compound. Three o'clock. The sun was getting lower in the sky, and the air was getting colder. It would soon be dark.

Max shivered. A sensation close to panic swept through him. He had spent most of his life in a tiny, well-ordered world of house, sheds, garden, and cow paddock. He'd never ventured beyond the boundary, even when there'd been no electric fence to stop him. But now, out here in the forest, he felt that he'd fallen off the world, into a wilderness unmapped, untamed, and unpredictable. It was an area too vast to contemplate. He could feel it pressing on him, crushing him from all sides.

He took a deep breath, smiled a wobbly smile, and hoisted Stefan into his arms. "After you."

For the first two hours they moved steadily, pushing through to the fire-access road and trotting once they were on it. But the going was rough and Stefan slowed them down. By five o'clock, when they began to look for shelter, they seemed to have traveled only a short distance.

Worries continued to crowd Max's mind. Freedom wasn't bringing a sense of relief and new possibilities, only confusion, guilt, and fear. He was struck by the immensity of what they'd done. Maybe he should have stayed inside the wire, where everything was explained, everything certain.

Half an hour later, Christina spotted a massive fallen tree, its trunk blackened and hollowed by a fire that must have swept through the area many years before. "How about here?"

Max looked at his watch. They had another thirty minutes of daylight left, but if they kept going they might find themselves in darkness and without shelter of any kind. "Perfect."

It wasn't perfect. Although the log was low and deep, one side was open to the elements. And to prowling animals, Max thought. While Christina scraped away the damp plants, moss, and toadstools growing within the shell of the tree, he collected dry leaves for a mattress and fashioned bristly twigs into a wall to seal the opening. He took Stefan with him, conscious that it was important to keep the boy stimulated.

After a while he began to find something satisfying about the work, the challenge. He had discovered a new side to himself in the generator shed and now was using it again. He began to whistle.

They perfected the shelter by the glow of the flashlight. The air was bitterly cold now, and with relief they crept onto the bed of leaves, closing the screen wall behind them. Max pointed the flashlight at his watch. "Six-thirty."

"Let's eat," Christina said, "then sleep, and start out again at first light."

"What do we have left?"

Christina reached into her pockets. "No water,"

she said sadly. "Only a bit of cheese, an apple, some bread, a packet of nuts and raisins." She tumbled everything into her lap.

Max leaned forward, shining the flashlight at the food. "And pocket fluff," he said.

Christina laughed in relief. If he could make jokes at a time like this, everything would be all right. "And one burnt match," she said, "and one button, slightly cracked."

"Delicious."

"Stef," Christina said, "are you hungry?"

Stefan coughed weakly, then sniffed. He didn't reply.

"Would you like a nice apple? Or some nuts?"

"We should all have some apple," Max said. "We need the juice, now that we've lost our water bottle."

Christina swallowed. She realized how dry her throat was. "Tomorrow we've got to get more supplies, even if it means stealing them."

Max nodded. He picked up the apple and polished it. Then he quartered it with the pocketknife and cut out the core. "Want yours peeled, Stef?"

Sniff. Stefan wasn't speaking again.

Max peeled two segments of the apple and offered them to him. "You have to eat, Stef. It'll make you feel better. We've got a long way to go tomorrow."

Stefan was breathing audibly, a tortured sound of congestion and unhappiness. His movements, when he finally ate the pieces of apple, were dull and spiritless.

"I wish he'd get his appetite back."

"Don't worry," Christina said. "With any luck we'll be somewhere safe tomorrow night."

"Hope so."

"Meanwhile, kind sir, what would you like for dinner?"

"I'll have roast bread with cheese sauce, followed by nut-and-raisin pie."

"Sounds divine."

They shared small portions of bread, cheese, nuts, and raisins, chewing slowly as though savoring the bland flavors.

Then, without warning, the bad feelings welled up in Max again. He began to cry, heaving helplessly. "What have we done? What's going to happen to us?"

Christina reached across and put her arms around his shoulders. "Shh. It's all right, it's all right."

"I'm scared."

Christina massaged his neck gently. "I am, too. But we'll find someone to help us. There must be records of who we are."

She continued to comfort him. Finally, drawn and exhausted, he said, "Let's sleep now."

They stretched out on the crackling leaves, Stefan burrowing into the warm gap between them. Damp, vegetably smells reached their nostrils from the ground and the furry burnt tree trunk. Snaps and scurries outside the shelter told of night animals beginning to hunt and scavenge for food. Max didn't think about that. He reached out to Christina in the darkness, curling his arm around her waist. She took his fingers in hers. She was very warm. He was asleep in minutes.

18

THEY WALKED for four hours the next morning. They were tired, dirty, thirsty, hungry. Their arms ached from carrying Stefan. Their nerves were on edge from his low, monotonous weeping.

But when they stumbled onto a paved road at eleven o'clock, their depression lifted at once. Shouting, "We made it," Christina tore out the last of her newspaper lining and began to cartwheel along the white line. Max, grinning so much his face ached, took Stefan's hands in his and danced in the center of the road. "Made it," he cried.

Stefan brightened a little. "Made it."

Christina settled breathlessly onto the grass at the side of the road. "Let's rest for a few minutes and finish the last of our food while we wait for a car."

Max frowned. "Better not. It might be ages be-fore we get more. We should save some."

She laughed up at his troubled face. "Typical. Mr. Caution. Okay, we'll save some of the nuts and raisins."

Max blushed and sat down next to her, holding Stefan in his lap. "I can't help it. It's just the way I am."

"It doesn't matter. In fact, we make a good team, you being cautious and me taking risks. We help each other."

They rested for ten minutes, nibbling at the last of the bread and the cheese. No vehicles passed them. Winds high in the atmosphere pushed cloud banks across the sky, so that they were alternately in sunlight and shadow. Exertion had kept them warm, but it had rained during the night and Max felt sure that more rain was due.

He grew uneasy. "We'll have to stay alert," he said. "Ratface or Sergeant Hanley could drive by."

Christina frowned. She hadn't thought of that. "Okay, whenever we hear a vehicle we'll hide. If it's safe we'll run out and wave it down."

She finished eating, brushed away the crumbs, and stood up. "But let's not wait here. I hate waiting."

Max looked up at her tangled blond hair and dirt-smudged cheeks. She's always impatient, he thought. "Which direction?"

She looked confused for a moment, then walked several meters to a stubby, white post. She looked at both sides of it, smiled at him, and pointed down the road in each direction. "The town of L is twenty-five kilometers that way," she said, "and the town of S is eight kilometers that way." She screwed up her nose at him. "What do *you* think?"

He grinned. "I think we should go to S."

They set out three abreast down the pitted, buckled tar road. They saw no signs of life, which Max found bewildering. Everything Ratface had told him about the world beyond the compound had created images in his head of cities teeming with grasping people, of highways choked with the headlong rush of traffic.

"It doesn't seem to be a very major road," he said, jumping over a large pothole. "Maybe that's why we haven't seen any traffic."

Christina skipped and windmilled her arms. "What do you think the 'S' stands for?"

"Stinkweed?" Max said. "Snotview?"

"Simpleton? Snitch?"

"Saturn? Sassafras?"

They shouted names to the sky. Stefan, infected with their high spirits, began to skip with them. "What do you think, Stef?" they said.

He paused, his thin, pale face looking from one of them to the other. "Slinger," he said softly.

Christina spun around. "Slingertown. What do you think happens in Slingertown?"

"Everyone goes around with worried faces," said Max.

"And horrible clothes."

"They're always apologizing."

"They eat grass and nuts."

The road stretched ahead of them through the forest, empty, twisting, but somehow promising hope. They walked for another hour, making up games, seeing no one, guided by the distance-markers. S7, S6, S5.

"Four kilometers to S," Christina said later. "That won't take us long."

She was leading the way. A hundred meters later, Max saw her stop, duck, and run at a crouch to the side of the road. Her hand warned them to keep down and get off the road.

She looked white and shocked when Max reached her.

"What's wrong?"

She pointed wordlessly among the trees. He half stood to get a better view.

There, in a clearing back from the road, was a small settlement. It consisted of a house, sheds, and vegetable gardens. A high wire fence surrounded it. Max saw telltale white knobs where the strands of wire met the posts.

Ceramic insulators. The fence was electrified. They had come upon another League compound.

"They're everywhere," said Christina shakily. She blinked back the tears in her eyes. "We haven't got a chance."

"Don't give up," Max said. He put his arm around her shoulders. "They don't own the world.

We can sneak past. We'll just be extra-careful from now on. We won't try to wave anyone down."

She leaned against him. "I was feeling so alive. Then this. It knocked the wind out of my sails."

"I know," he said. "Me too."

They were interrupted by a desolate keening behind them. Stefan had seen the electric fence.

19

"YOU CARRY HIM," Christina said. "My arms are tired."

"I carried him last time. It's your turn."

"Yeah, sure."

Christina bundled Stefan into her arms. "We should have hidden it from him. One glimpse of that place and he's all hopeless again."

They were approaching the three-kilometer post, hugging the edge of the road, ready to duck among the trees at the first sign of an approaching vehicle. So far they had seen only one, a massive, unstoppable truck, loaded with tree trunks. The town of S lay ahead, but it was an unknown. What would they do when they got there? Who could they trust? The trouble was, even if the League controlled every town and every road, there was no other way out. They'd have to risk it.

It took them an hour to reach the outskirts. By then Stefan was a dead weight in their arms, his body limp, his eyes vacant, a sob escaping from him every few seconds.

They entered the town warily, coming upon a picnic area first, then neat fences, distant buildings, road signs, and billboards.

"Take-out food, 100 meters on the right," read Max. He looked about him, curious and alert. His earlier fears had vanished. Being in this strange new place made him tingle with anticipation. He wanted to know how these people lived their lives. He wanted to know what they thought and felt.

"Welcome to Sunnyglen," Christina said, pointing to a road sign. "Not the sort of name the League would use."

Max grinned. "They'd call it *Rainy*glen."

"Gloomyview."

"Miseryburg."

Encouraged, they entered the town. It consisted of a main shopping street flanked by two or three small streets of plain white clapboard cottages. The shops were single-story brick buildings with veranda fronts. Some rusty, mud-splashed cars and pickup trucks were parked along the main street. A huge logging truck idled in front of a distant service station. Beyond it, a railroad track ran past the squat smokestack of a sawmill. Taking all this in, Christina said, "It's a lumber town."

"It's huge," Max said.

Christina scoffed. "Huge? This? This is nothing. Wait till you see the city."

Max blushed. He hated being ignorant about the world. "As long as it's got food."

"What would you like?"

"A hamburger. I've wanted to try one ever since you told me about them."

"My mouth is watering," Christina said. "We have to try to act normally from now on, like we belong or we're visitors."

Before approaching any of the shops they brushed the dry mud and leaves from their clothes and combed their hair with their fingers. Max wet a corner of his handkerchief and cleaned the dirt from Christina's cheeks. She stiffened, watching him with a complicated expression. Then she relaxed, smiling as if they were alone together, and safe.

It was early afternoon now. Adults were at work, children were in school. Apart from one or two women with shopping baskets in the baker's and the grocer's, the street was deserted.

They drew near a small take-out food shop. Steel trays of fish cakes, chips, and hot dogs steamed inside the window. Smells compounded of salt, vinegar, and fried food drifted through the doorway.

Max was fascinated. He hadn't known that such places existed. Were you allowed simply to go in and ask for whatever food you wanted? Dizzy with hunger, he put his face to the window and peered up at the blackboard above the grills. "Plain hamburgers, two dollars fifty. With toppings, four dollars. Do we have enough for a plain hamburger each?"

Christina released Stefan's hand and searched in her pockets for the money she'd pilfered from Slinger and Moaner over the years. She brought out some coins and crumpled bills. "Plenty," she said. "About twelve dollars."

"Stef? Do you want a hamburger? Delicious."

The little boy's face was masklike. His shoulders drooped. It was as if all the rapid changes of the past two days had been too much for him and he'd stopped reacting to things. The sooner they got him to a doctor, or his home, the better.

"Stef?" said Max coaxingly. "Are you hungry? Would you like a hamburger?"

The cook was looking at them curiously through the shop window. Christina tugged Max's sleeve. "Let's buy him a hamburger anyway," she said. "Food will bring him back to life."

Max looked at her in embarrassment. "I've never bought anything before. You'll have to do all the talking."

"Okay."

They trooped into the shop.

"You look like you've been playing in the dirt," the man said. "No school today?"

Max opened and closed his mouth.

Christina said quickly, "We're moving to a new place to live. We got dirty packing. Our mum and dad are getting gas."

The man shrugged. It was of no interest to him what other people did. "What would you like?"

"Three plain hamburgers, please."

They watched his every move—cutting open the buns, turning the beef patties on the grill, stirring onions with the spatula. The cooking smells rose and coiled about their nostrils. Finally the man bagged their hamburgers and frowned as he added the charges in his head. "It's seven dollars fifty altogether."

Solemnly, almost unable to conceal her haste, Christina passed the man two one-dollar notes and three two-dollar notes.

"You must be kidding," the man said.

Christina didn't understand. "You said seven-fifty. I gave you eight dollars."

The man lifted the notes as if they were unclean. He had a gray, cynical, dissatisfied face. "I can't accept these. They went out of circulation last year, replaced by coins. Maybe I could exchange them at the bank, but it's a hassle." He reached his arm protectively around the three hamburgers. "Have you got enough coins, or a couple of five-dollar notes there?"

Christina looked hot-faced at the remaining money in her hand. The notes were useless. She counted the coins slowly: ninety cents, a dollar ten, dollar twenty, dollar fifty, two dollars . . . two dollars fifty!

"I've got two dollars fifty in coins," she said. She stacked them on the counter and held out her hand. "Can we have just one hamburger?"

The man was disgusted. "What about the other two I've made? That's good food wasted, that is. That's five dollars down the drain. Do you think I'm made of money? Why don't you get the right money from your parents?"

Christina had had enough of this. She snatched a hamburger from his grasp, shouted, "Eat the others yourself, fatguts!" and hurried out of the shop, pushing Stefan and Max ahead of her.

They burst onto the sidewalk, looked wildly in both directions, then ran down an alley at the side of the supermarket. Angry shouts trailed behind them. They crossed the small parking lot at the rear of the supermarket, ducked through a hole in the fence, and ran to the shelter of an abandoned car.

"Phew," Christina said, alarmed and excited at the same time. Then she snorted once or twice, trying to hold in her laughter.

Max let go first. He held his stomach, laughing hard and spluttering, *"Eat them yourself, fatguts."*

"Do you think I'm made of money?" Christina snorted.

"Money down the drain."

Only Stefan was unaffected. While they joked,

contorted with laughter, he stood listlessly, as if he were not part of the world around him.

Christina suddenly sobered. She had glimpsed his long, pale face. She felt something snap inside her. "What's wrong with you?" she shouted, shaking his shoulders. "Wake up. Say something."

Max grasped her arms. "Hold on. You know he's sick. In fact, I think we should take him to a doctor."

Christina turned on him. "Well, we can't. What if it's a League doctor? We'd be turned over to Ratface again."

Max looked away, avoiding the force of her fears and anxiety. "Okay, forget it. Let's eat."

Muttering about everyone slowing her down, Christina tore the hamburger into three parts. She ate her share quickly, looking out across the railroad tracks, too angry and frustrated to pay attention to the others.

Max hated these mood swings of hers. Quietly, so that he wouldn't draw attention to himself, he knelt down and put his arm around Stefan. "Here, Stef," he whispered. "Nice hamburger."

Stefan blinked but was otherwise still. Max broke Stefan's share of the hamburger into smaller pieces. "Try this," he said softly.

After a few seconds, Stefan let himself be fed. He chewed halfheartedly. Max saw him swallow. So far, so good, he thought. Now we need something to drink.

He stood up. This was a run-down part of the

town. Weeds grew high in the ditches along the railroad tracks. Two cats were crouching at the edge of an overturned rubbish bin. On the other side of a broad stretch of empty ground were the backyards of several houses. External plumbing braced the walls; palings were missing from the fences.

It was a sorry-looking corner of the world they'd come to. That didn't seem right to Max. From everything Ratface had told him, the world was obsessed with money and possessions. He had dim memories of bedtime rhymes and stories about city streets paved with gold. There was a huge gap, he suspected, between the real world and the White League's version of it. He wanted to trust his eyes, but it was hard to shake off the things he'd been told for so many years.

Then Christina spoke. "I'm sorry, Max. Sorry, Stef."

Max turned to her in relief. "It doesn't matter. We've had too many scares lately."

"What are we going to do now?"

"First we should drink something," he said. "Then we should move on. See that house over there? The one with the mattress hanging over the back fence? There's a tap by the gate."

They set off across the empty ground, looking back often at the alleys leading to the main street. They didn't want the hamburger cook chasing them with his greasy knives.

Someone had placed a dented metal dish under

the tap. Spiky clawprints crisscrossed the muddy dirt around it. Hens! Max felt a sudden rush of longing for the farm, the uncomplicated life inside the compound. He turned on the tap, cupped his hands under the stream of water, and sipped experimentally. Cool, clean, faintly metallic. He drank thirstily.

A voice said, "You want a glass of milk? Lemonade? Something to eat?"

Max jumped. A jolt of panic slammed through him like a charge of electricity. He recovered, jerked away from the tap, half-crouched as if to flee.

A girl of Stefan's age was watching them. "My father says, You want a real drink? Are you hungry?"

Max sensed Stefan and Christina creep closer to him. He enveloped one in each arm and the three fugitives stood staring back at the girl. The girl frowned a little, seeming puzzled by their alarm. She had a round face, black straight hair, skin the color of cinnamon. An Asian! Max thought. It was in all the White League's booklets, the crudely drawn comic strips: Asian people and black people were a threat to the Supreme Line. They were driven by envy. Ratface said they couldn't be trusted.

Max stepped back, dragging the others with him. "*Run!*" he whispered urgently.

The child came through the open gate now. Her arms were cradling a sleeping puppy. It was fat, black, and furry, and Stefan let out a little cry of need: "Oh."

He darted forward. He began to stroke the puppy, soft, inexpert pats on its head and spine.

Then Christina released herself from Max's encircling arm. She smiled at the child, and she and Stefan stood side by side, stroking the puppy. Max looked on helplessly.

He glanced over the fence toward the house. A man was watching them from a garden chair. He'd been reading a newspaper. There was a small table at his elbow, set with a cup of coffee, a bowl of sugar, a plate of cookies. A milky glass was next to the sugar bowl. Max looked back at the girl. Sure enough, there was a smudge of milk on her upper lip.

This was hard for Max. The resistance he had felt was automatic. He'd never met anyone of another race before, but hatred and fear had been drummed into him in a gloomy classroom for most of his life. Now he was being forced to ask, Has the White League been wrong about this, too?

The man got up from his chair, went into the house. Max stiffened: what did it mean? The man reappeared. Max breathed a sigh of relief. The man was carrying three glasses, a cookie jar, and a jug of lemonade, and he was smiling shyly. The little girl saw him and grinned, and when he stood next to her she gazed at Max, Christina, and Stefan calmly, without fear. She feels secure, she feels loved, Max realized with a pang. He saw that she had something he didn't have, something he wanted more than anything in the world.

When the man spoke it was softly, musically, in another language. The girl translated: "My father says you must have something to eat and something to drink."

And so they had a small party there, around the back gate. The man smiled often, urging them to eat more cookies. He made no effort to question them through his daughter. And when they left finally, setting out to find the highway again, he made no effort to detain them. Max wondered about that. The man seemed to understand their predicament, as if he'd been through the same things himself. Max tried to imagine the man's past life. Maybe he'd fled a country where people were forced to give up their homes and fend for themselves. It was a new experience for Max, attempting to see things from the point of view of a person he'd been told he should distrust and hate.

They made their way along a grid of small streets to the other side of the town. There was the buckled road again. It stretched, empty and unpromising, between forest and grazing land.

"We need to hurry," Max said. "The hamburger man could be telephoning the police by now. He might know Sergeant Hanley. We have to get as far away as possible, and no hitchhiking."

Christina groaned. "Yes, boss." They had experienced ten minutes of kindness, but now their old fears were returning. Nothing had changed. Were they going to walk and hide forever?

20

THEY TRUDGED for eight kilometers that afternoon, passing a tiny church and cemetery, old
shacks, distant farmhouses. There was no sign of
life. Then, in mid-afternoon, the road seemed to fill
with traffic and they found themselves in a state of
constant panic, walking a few hundred meters, then
dashing into the bushes, walking, dashing into the
bushes.

Mothers were driving children in some of the
cars; other cars were driven by tired-looking men
wearing work clothes. Max was bewildered. Where
were these people going? Christina knew more
about life on the outside than he did. "Who are
they?" he asked.

"Kids being collected from school. Lumber
workers driving home from work."

Max stared at them suspiciously. He began to gain an impression of the pace of life in the outside world—the routine, the hurry, the bewildering diversity. An odd apprehension settled in him. If my father passed in a car, would I know him? If my grandmother served me in a shop, would I know her? What if my mother lived in the next street all my life and never recognized me, never met me? And I could walk right past the gravestones of my ancestors and never know it.

At half past five the traffic eased, but the sun had dipped below the tree-lined horizon. Rain began to fall. They half walked, half ran, searching the road's edge for shelter.

Just as they were about to settle for a dripping space under a tree, they came to a crossroads marked with a signpost. The intersecting road was a major one, broad and well marked. A hundred meters down stood a small glass-and-cement structure. Max pointed. "What's that?"

"Don't know," Christina said. "But I don't intend to stand out here getting wet."

Max glanced at the signpost. It read OAKBANK 120. He followed Christina at a run, Stefan in his arms. At each jarring step he heard the boy wheezing.

Christina reached the shelter and swung out again. "A bus stop," she said excitedly. "That's how we'll get away. We'll catch a bus."

Max helped Stefan stretch out on the bench

seat. Catch a bus? Was it the same as buying a hamburger? He peered at the timetable. It was water-stained, unreadable. Strange words had been spray-painted on the walls. "Won't we need money?"

"Doesn't matter. We'll say our parents are paying at the other end. When we get there we'll run off before the driver can stop us."

"What if he won't let us aboard?"

"What if, what if, what if," said Christina. "Why can't you just think positive for a change instead of worrying what if, what if, what if? Of *course* he'll pick us up. Three kids at night in the rain, of *course* he'll pick us up. Gawd."

She flung herself onto the bench next to Stefan, her arms folded.

With a sigh, Max leaned against the plexiglass wall of the shelter. Now and then, as headlights appeared in the distance, Christina stepped out, ready to hail a bus.

Six o'clock. Half past six. There was no moonlight. Dense, low rainclouds were banked in the sky. Rain continued to fall—steady, drenching, monotonous. Everyone's at home, Max thought, eating hamburgers in front of a warm fire. No one but three runaway kids would be crazy enough to be out in this weather. He felt a twinge of guilt for subjecting Stefan to the cold and rain. He wondered, for the hundredth time, whether they should return to the compound, to a way of life that was certain and secure. Life out here on the outside was risky and unpredictable. If freedom meant having to make endless decisions and anticipate endless dangers, was it worth it? The White League protected you from all that.

He was about to say to Christina, "This is hopeless," when a car swished by slowly in the rain. It stopped a hundred meters past them, then began to reverse.

"Uh oh," Max said. He watched nervously. It was a plain white car. Ratface had a white car.

The white sedan drew alongside the bus stop. The passenger door opened and a woman's voice said, "Oh, you poor things."

She got out and hurried toward them, hunched over in the slanting rain. She had fair hair and a kind, concerned face, like the man and the little girl in the car behind her. "You poor things," said the woman again. "The last bus was at a quarter to six."

Christina got to her feet, staring warily at the woman and then at the car. We'll have to play this carefully, she thought. We have to seem like normal kids. She threw up her arms as if in despair. "Oh, no! We must've just missed it."

"You can't stay here," the woman said.

Her husband got out of the car and joined her. "Hop in. We'll give you a lift."

"Yes," said the woman, nodding vigorously. "Are you going far?"

Max remembered the signpost. "We're going to Oakbank."

"Oakbank? That's a long way," the woman said. She turned to her husband. "What do you think, dear? They're going to Oakbank."

The man frowned. "Oakbank. It would take us three or four hours, there and back, in this rain, at this time of the evening."

"Oh dear," the woman said. "Is anyone meeting you? Won't they be worried?"

Thinking quickly, Christina said, "Mum's in the hospital, so we're going to stay with our uncle."

"We'd better telephone him," the man said.

"He hasn't got a phone," said Christina.

Max, she thought. *Help me, please.*

"Oh dear," said the woman again. "He'll be very worried when he sees you're not on the bus. Perhaps we should tell the police."

Max stepped in at last. "We go there every weekend," he said. "He knows we'll arrive tonight or tomorrow morning. He lives close to the bus stop, so we always walk to his place and let ourselves in." He patted his pocket. "We've got the key. No problem."

Christina watched the frowns on the faces of the man and the woman. They doubt our story, she thought, and I don't blame them. Or maybe they're horrified at such casual behavior. She was grateful to Max. Under the circumstances, it was the best story they could have concocted to explain their presence on this miserable road, on this miserable night.

But what now? If we say we'll walk home again they'll want to take us.

As if reading her thoughts, the man said, "Hop in. We'd better take you back to your place."

Christina looked at him, all her senses alert. I can't trust these people yet, she thought. I don't know enough about them. She said quickly, "Our dad's gone away for a few days. The house is all closed up."

The man clicked his tongue. "Terrible," he said, "letting children look after themselves in weather like this.

"Terrible," agreed his wife. "I know—would you like to spend the night with us. We've got a little dairy farm near here. We'll take you to the bus in the morning. Poor things, you look so cold and wet."

She stepped forward to peer at Stefan, who lay unblinking on the bench seat. They heard her breathe in sharply. She turned and said, "But this child's sick!"

"Let me see," the man said. He stepped past Max and Christina. "Poor little fellow. We'll take him home and put him right to bed." He lifted Stefan off the seat. "He should never have been allowed out in weather like this. Dear oh dear."

Tut-tutting angrily, he carried Stefan to the car. The little girl, silent and immobile all this time, opened her door and scooted back along the seat, making room for Stefan.

"In you go," the woman said, ushering Max and Christina to the car.

Max sat between the two adults. He watched curiously as the man started the engine, turned on the lights, released the hand brake, and shifted the gear lever from PARK to DRIVE. He had never seen a gear lever like that before. Slinger's farm truck had a lever marked 1, 2, 3, 4 and R.

Christina sat in the backseat. She smiled at the little girl, who ducked her head shyly.

As they pulled away from the bus stop, the woman said, "I'm Mrs. Ellis and this is Mr. Ellis, and our daughter is called Albina."

Christina pointed. "That's Max, this is Stefan, and I'm Christina."

They all lapsed into silence, listening to the windshield wipers sweeping away the rain. A few minutes later, the man said suddenly, "Where's your luggage?"

"We keep spare clothes at our aunt's place," Christina said.

"Aunt? I thought you said you were staying with your uncle."

"Aunt and uncle," Max said quickly.

"Humph," said Mr. Ellis. He didn't sound convinced.

Christina's heart was hammering. They're very worried about us, she thought. Shall I tell them who we are? Can I risk it?

Beside her, Stefan shifted with the movement of the car. Soon his head was in her lap and he slept,

Harvey Two clasped to his chest. She looked across at the little girl. She, too, had fallen asleep.

And Christina and Max slept. After their cold night in the forest, and the shocks and reversals and hunger of the day, the car's interior seemed to hold them in a cocoon of warmth and security.

21

THEY SLEPT for twenty minutes, then woke with a jerk when the car bumped gently into a garage. The hand brake clicked on.

"Home," the woman said, turning to smile at Christina and Stefan. "A hot bath first, I think, then into some dry clothes, then supper, then bed."

"You're very kind," said Max.

A small wooden door led to the kitchen from the garage. As they filed into the house, Christina looked back, unsettled by the moaning of the wind. Through the open garage door she glimpsed impenetrable darkness and slanting rain, nothing else. She shivered.

Then she was inside the house. The kitchen was

plain and uncluttered, a place of warmth and peace. They swept through to another door and into a long corridor, Mrs. Ellis ahead of them, clicking on the lights, Mr. Ellis behind them, hanging the car keys on a hook by the back door, saying "You'll soon be warm and dry."

They came to a large spare bedroom with three single beds in it. The walls were painted white. On the floor was a fluffy rug, the only sign of extravagance that Christina had seen so far. But it's a nice place, she thought, and they're nice people.

While Christina soaked in a bath in the main bathroom, Max and Stefan were taken to a small shower next to the laundry room at the back of the house. When they returned to the bedroom, they found that their damp, dirty clothes had been taken away and replaced by old, clean, well-darned trousers, shirts, and sweaters.

Christina was already dressed, in a heavy woolen skirt and top. She had washed and combed her hair. It hung in dark gold strands to her shoulders. "What do you think?" she asked, when Max and Stefan had finished dressing.

"About what?"

"This place. Mr. and Mrs. Ellis."

"They seem nice. I think we should tell them who we are and ask them to help us."

"I agree."

Then footsteps sounded in the corridor. Christina quickly leaned close to Max. She smelt subtly of soap. Her breath was warm in his ear. "We'll tell them in the morning," she whispered. "Not now. It's too much for them to take in now."

He nodded. He turned briefly to look at her. Her face was very close. She kissed him fleetingly, then stepped away from him.

There was a tap on the door. "Come in," they called.

The door opened. Mrs. Ellis's smiling face looked in. "Feel better?" She entered the room and placed pajamas at the foot of their beds. She looked closely at Stefan. "You certainly look happier, my dear. Ready for your supper?"

Stefan hid his face against Christina's skirt. Mrs. Ellis smiled. "This way."

They followed her to a darkened sitting room. A fire burned in the grate, providing a warm, soft light. A sofa and two armchairs faced the fireplace. A coffee table on the hearth rug had been set with bowls of soup and mugs of hot milk. There was no sign of Albina, but Mr. Ellis rose from one of the armchairs. "This will warm your insides," he said, gesturing at the coffee table.

They sat together on the sofa and stared into the fire while they ate. Mr. and Mrs. Ellis looked on, smiling and nodding approvingly. Little was said. An old clock ticked on the mantelpiece. The world outside was dark and troubled, sheets of rain beating against the windows and the wind groaning in the trees, but inside they felt warm and safe. *Tick, tock, tick, tock*. Soon Stefan was asleep against Max's shoulder.

Mrs. Ellis said softly, "Time for bed."

She showed them back to their room and gave them each a quick, shy kiss. After a few minutes they heard footsteps going to and from the bathroom. Lights were clicked off. The house settled into sleep.

When Max awoke some time later, he lay still for a moment, listening. Something had woken him, but he didn't know what. He listened: wind, scudding rain, the creaks and groans that all houses make.

And something else.

A soft voice, that was it. He crept to the bedroom door. Holding himself tensely, he turned the handle and pushed the door open a couple of centimeters. The voice was louder now.

It was Mr. Ellis. He was talking on the hall phone. "Yes," he was saying, "it's definitely them. You were right about the names: Christina, Max, Stefan . . . No, they're asleep now. . . . You'll collect them in the morning? Fine. Good-bye. In the League is strength."

22

"IT'S NOT FAIR," Christina said. "It's just not fair."

She began to cry softly, then gathered herself to glare at Max in the dim light of their flashlight. "Are you sure? I didn't see anything when we came in, did you? They seem like nice people, not League members."

"Shh," Max said, glancing nervously across at the door. "Slinger and Moaner would seem nice, too, if you were meeting them for the first time," he whispered. "It's Ratface. They all do what he tells them to do."

Christina flopped back on her pillow. "He probably ordered the whole mountain to watch out for us. What are we going to do?"

Max got up from the edge of her bed. He'd come to some rapid conclusions since overhearing Mr. Ellis on the telephone, but they were conclusions Christina would not want to hear. He hovered awkwardly on the fluffy rug, looking down at her.

"Well?" she demanded. "What now?"

"This is it," he said helplessly. "They've got us."

Christina's eyes narrowed. She sprang out of bed. "No!"

"But what can we do? They're everywhere; we don't know how to get out of this house; we can't look after Stefan properly—"

"He's not that sick," Christina said. "If he stays in the League's hands, he'll get worse."

"All right, all right," Max said, to shut her up. "But we've got no plan, no supplies, no transportation—except on foot in the rain," he added sarcastically.

Christina folded her arms. "We'll steal their car."

"Steal their car? Who's going to drive—you? Get real, Christina. Stop dreaming."

He regretted the words as soon as he said them, but he had a perverse desire to get back at her.

Christina advanced on him, her voice low and dangerous. "Dreaming got us this far. If we give up now it will be the same as giving up forever. We'll lose our pasts. We'll forget everything. Our minds will be theirs. We'll become just like them inside. We'll never know if our mothers or fathers are alive. Is that what you want?"

"No. But—"

"But what?"

"It's too much for us," said Max miserably. "You never consider the *how* of anything. How are we going to steal their car? We don't even know where the keys are."

He pushed back his hair. This was like a bad, familiar dream. Perhaps I'll wake up in a minute, he thought.

"Listen to me," Christina said sharply. "The keys are on a hook by the back door. This is our only chance. You can drive his car, can't you?"

Max considered his options. A part of him had lost heart. If they returned to the White League, all responsibilities would be passed back to Ratface. No more doubts and anxieties.

Then he caught himself. Did he have the right to make decisions for Stefan and Christina? No. Besides, if they returned to the White League, Christina would shut him out of her life. Eventually she'd escape. Stefan would be lost, too. Ratface would mold him, make a puppet out of him.

And we've done well up till now, Max thought. I don't want to lose Christina. I don't want to give up on Stefan. I want freedom, not a life with the League.

He forced himself to concentrate. This was real: it wasn't a dream. "I watched him start the engine," he said slowly, "but the gears are different." He frowned. "What about the fence, the gate?"

"We'll ram our way through."

He was alarmed. Steal someone else's car? Wreck their property? "Ram?" he said.

"Yep." Christina knifed the air with the side of her hand. "Straight through. It's the only way."

Her eyes gleamed. She likes the idea, Max thought. To her, this is fun.

Christina turned away and stripped off her pajama top. He saw her warm, bare back. He felt confused. He stood watching the tendons flex beneath the surface of her skin.

"Don't just stand there," she said, her voice muffled by the old sweater she was tangled in.

Did she have eyes in the back of her head? The spell broken, Max unbottoned his pajamas and began to get dressed. Behind him, Christina was gently waking Stefan. We always seem to be starting, Max thought. One day we'll finish.

He crossed the room and helped Christina drag the trousers, sweater, and parka on over Stefan's pajamas. Stefan was still half-asleep, his body compliant.

Then he jerked suddenly. "I'm going to throw up."

Christina held his shoulders, and they watched helplessly as he vomited hamburger, soup, and milk onto the fluffy carpet. He wailed and gulped. His stomach heaved.

When the spasm was over, Max cleaned Stefan's hot face with his handkerchief.

144

"He needs a doctor."

Christina snapped, "I know. But not yet. When we're somewhere safe."

"Sooner than that."

"No. We can't trust anyone."

"I'll take him myself," said Max stubbornly. "At the first town we come to."

"We stick together," Christina said. "We need each other. And that's final."

She was looking at her watch as she spoke. "It's only ten o'clock. We can't risk leaving yet."

They waited until eleven o'clock, getting back into bed fully dressed in case someone came to check on them. When it was time to leave, Max wrapped Stefan and Harvey Two in a blanket while Christina listened at the door for sounds in the dark corridor outside their room. The squalling wind and rain made it difficult for her to hear anything, but she knew it would cover their footsteps and whispering. She beckoned.

"We'll go out the back way," she said, her lips brushing Max's ear. "That way we can collect the car keys and avoid going past their bedrooms. Then right to the car."

The rain-laden wind lashed them the instant they stepped outside of the house. They leaned into it, supporting each other, their clothes blown flat against their bodies. It was the blackest of nights. Max had an impression of neat garden beds, a hose across a path, and whipping wet branches, but not of anything a meter beyond their stumbling feet.

They turned a corner, cutting off the wind. "Down here," Christina said, leading them beside the garage wall.

They turned another corner. Max's night vision was sharper now. They were at the entrance to the garage. Inside it was the car, a large, forbidding shape in the darkness.

"Here goes nothing," he said, unlocking the doors.

Christina lay Stefan along the backseat, wrapped in the blanket. By crossing the seat belts she was able to strap him in securely. Then she got into the front, where Max was holding the steering wheel, his knuckles white and tense.

"What if I make a mistake?" he said.

Christina touched his wrist. "I'll help. We'll work it out together. First, see if you can remember what Mr. Ellis did when he started the car at the bus stop."

Max had his door partly open to keep the interior light on. The dials and switches and gauges faced him, mute and oppressive. He waggled the steering wheel a little.

Christina pointed at the gear lever. "Where was this?"

"Where it is now. In PARK."

"Where did he put it after he started the car?"

"In DRIVE."

"DRIVE must mean forward. Don't you dare put

it in DRIVE, or we'll crash through the wall. You'll have to put it in REVERSE. What else did he do?"

Max's hands were shaking. "He started the engine."

"Do it."

Max turned the key gingerly. At once little lights came on and the fuel gauge slowly swung round to register half-full. But no engine sounds.

"Turn it more."

The engine erupted into life. It seemed to roar.

"Make it go quieter!" said Christina in alarm.

Max took his hands from the steering wheel as if that might help. "I'm not doing anything. It's doing it itself."

After a moment, the engine settled into a gentler rhythm.

"Now what?" Christina said.

Max peered at the switches and turned on the headlights. Garden rakes and tools seemed to spring at him from the walls of the shed. He pulled his door closed.

"Gawd," Christina muttered. "We'll wake the whole mountain at this rate." She pointed at a red light on the dashboard. "It says BRAKE."

"Hand brake," said Max in relief. He leaned down and released the hand brake. He looked at Christina for encouragement, shifted the gear lever into REVERSE, and prodded the accelerator with his foot.

The car shot out of the shed. It plowed back over

garden beds in a series of mad charges. Christina was flung around in her seat. She braced her hands on the dashboard. "Can't . . . you . . . drive . . . more . . . gently?"

Then her jaws closed with a click. They had backed up against a tree. The rear wheels spun freely in the mud as Max, transfixed with panic, continued to push down on the accelerator.

"Change gears." Christina shouted. "Gawd, we haven't got time for knocking down firewood."

She reached out and clicked the gear lever into DRIVE. The car leapt forward, Max steering wildly, overcorrecting every mistake. They sideswiped garden taps and bushes. The headlights swooped drunkenly over the rain-slicked trees.

Just as Max was getting accustomed to steering the willful car, a fence and a gate loomed over them.

"*Go!*" said Christina. "*Straight through!*"

She pressed down on his knee. The car charged ahead.

Max closed his eyes as the gate rushed at them. At the last moment he realized that the gate and the fence were made of wood. He thought irrelevantly, Perhaps not everyone in the White League is afraid of outsiders. Then there were sounds of splintering and tearing.

They were through.

23

CHRISTINA WHOOPED: "Made it!"

You said that once before, Max thought sourly. The hard part's not over yet.

They were rushing headlong into the black night and he feared the unknown shapes at the edge of the road. He eased his foot off the accelerator to slow the car.

When that didn't help, he braked.

Too hard. The nose of the car dipped. Suddenly they were thrown sideways in their seats as the car spun 180 degrees on the wet surface and stopped.

"Well, that's one way of turning around," Christina said shakily. "Now where?"

Max restarted the engine. He took a deep breath to calm himself. "I thought you had a plan all worked out," he said.

"All I know is, when they report this car stolen we'll be caught in no time—"

"Great," Max said. "Now you tell me."

"—so we're going to hide the car," Christina continued, "and sneak aboard a train."

Max started to argue with her automatically, but then he paused, remembering that Christina knew about these things. "Do you think we can?" he asked.

"We saw a railroad track at Sunnyglen," she said impatiently. "With any luck we'll meet the track again somewhere, follow it to a town, park the car in a dark corner, and get onto a train. Plenty of hiding places on a train."

"Do trains run this late?"

"Questions, questions, questions," she said. "If there's no train we'll sleep in the car and catch a morning train. No one will look for the car in a station parking lot."

Max frowned. "Don't we need tickets? I read about it in a story once, about this kid who had to get off the train because she didn't have a ticket."

Christina wasn't in the mood for his doubts and fears. She pointed into the darkness. "Go."

No driving examiner would have given Max a license after seeing his performance that night. The car seemed to surge and brake inexplicably. It swerved left and right. The highway was deserted, and they hoped it would remain that way.

Twenty minutes later, when lights appeared ahead, Max began to slow the car. They'd come to the outskirts of a town called Blackwood. According to a sign, there was a train station on the other side of it.

The town also had a traffic light. It was changing from yellow to red. Max let the car creep toward the intersection, trying to stop without another wild spin. Beside him, Christina hung grimly to her seatbelt.

Then he sensed her draw back, breathe in sharply, and open her mouth to shout a warning. A Greyhound bus had appeared on their right. It entered the intersection, spraying oily water like a massive, wallowing creature of the sea.

There was a terrible pause while Max pressed the brake. He couldn't judge the pressure. The car edged over the white line. The bus loomed. A horn blared.

Then the bus was past, disappearing into its own mist.

"Gawd," Christina said. "Who taught *you* to drive?" She peered into the darkness. "Left. The station's on our left."

The road surface was slick, washed with reflections from the streetlights and neon signs of the town. They passed shops and several houses.

One house, set farther back from the others, had a blue lamp on a pole near the front door. "That's a doctor's office," Max said, slowing the car to read the sign on the front of the building. "We could take Stef in to be treated."

"Forget it. We're catching a train."

Max sighed. He drove on. A minute later, they came upon the station. It was still brightly lit. Shadowy figures moved around on the platform. He steered off the street and into the parking lot, creeping past parked cars to a distant corner where trees and a hedge blocked light from the street and the station buildings.

He braked and turned off the engine. "Looks like a train is due."

Christina unbuckled her seat belt. "Good. We'll hide in a sleeper."

"Sleeper? What's that?"

"Some cars are divided into little compartments with fold-down beds. I traveled in one when I was little."

She got out of the car and opened the back door to wake Stefan. Max hovered behind her. "Is he all right?"

"No change."

"Maybe the doctor can give him some pills before we catch the train."

"At this hour? Do you want us to miss the train?"

"I could say it's an emergency."

Christina backed away from the open door and turned around. "Max," she said firmly, "this is the last stage. Don't wreck it. If you want to do something useful, see if there's anything in the car we can scrounge."

She turned back to finish unstrapping Stefan, hating herself a little. It's the tension, she told herself. It's making us short-tempered. Things will improve soon.

"A five-dollar note," Max said.

"Better than nothing. Okay, let's go."

"Is it enough to buy a ticket?"

"Max," said Christina, "we are going to hide on the train, okay? Stop being such a worrier."

Max blushed. He took Stefan's hand and followed Christina into the building. According to his watch the time was fifteen minutes to midnight. Above the ticket counter were a clock and a sign that said NEXT TRAIN. The hands of the clock stood at 11:50—the train was due in five minutes.

"Just in time," Christina said. She glanced around nervously at the people waiting on the platform—a bored-looking woman, three young men with backpacks, and a large, emotional family clustered around an elderly uncle or grandfather.

"We should wait at the end of the platform," Max whispered, "where no one will notice us."

"That's exactly where we would be noticed," Christina replied. "If we stand here with everyone else, we'll blend in."

She saw Max look doubtfully at their old, ill-fitting clothes and at the sensible traveling clothes worn by the other passengers. He shrugged. "Suit yourself."

They sensed rather than heard the train's approach. Everyone on the platform seemed to stop talking at once, look down the track, and listen. A distant light shimmered in the darkness. For a long time, the light appeared to be motionless.

Then the train was upon them, advancing through the station, the diesel engine throbbing, the cars heaving *ba-bump ba-bump* over the tracks. Max trembled, drawing back in fear. The train loomed like a snarling beast, poisoning the air, shaking the world apart. He imagined the iron wheels cutting him in two. He closed his eyes, Stefan clasping his legs tightly.

Christina saw their terror. She put her arms around them and watched the passing cars closely. Blinds were drawn on most of the windows, but when the sleeper cars passed she saw that some compartments were empty.

The train heaved to a stop. A sleepy-looking man alighted. The waiting passengers pressed forward. Above them, the loudspeaker crackled into life: "The train on Platform 1 leaves in three minutes. The train on Platform 1 leaves in three minutes."

Max opened his eyes and let out a ragged, relieved breath. He was safe, but he couldn't imagine riding in this noisy box of metal and glass. "Boy," he said.

"Car 5," said Christina softly, catching his arm. "It's a sleeper. We'll have a better chance of avoiding people there."

"Suit yourself."

Christina looked at him sharply. "It's going to be okay, Max. It's only a train."

She saw him nod dubiously. Sighing, she led them to the door farthest from the conductor's compartment. They climbed aboard and shut the door. The train seemed to hum and mutter, as though veins and nerves ran through it. Stefan coughed softly and ceaselessly in Max's arms.

"Wait here," Christina said, "while I fetch some water for him."

She made her way into the next car. Set in the wall near the connecting door was a chrome tap and a rack of disposable cups. She filled one of the cups and returned to Car 5.

The corridor was empty.

She rushed to the window and looked out. Max was hurrying along the platform with Stefan in his arms. She watched them push by passengers still saying their farewells and enter the main station building. She looked at her watch. Two minutes left.

Then it was one minute.

She was paralyzed with indecision.

Thirty seconds.

Fifteen.

There was no sign of Max or Stefan. The whistle blew. The train lurched. Christina hovered at the door. Beneath her, the clacketing wheels began to pick up speed.

24

CHRISTINA wrapped her arms about herself for comfort. She felt betrayed and angry. She knew what had happened. Max's first loyalty had been to Stefan. He was probably banging on the doctor's door this very minute. Idiot, she thought. Doesn't he know they'll be in Ratface's hands by morning? Doesn't he know Stefan will be worse off then? Doesn't he care about himself? Doesn't he care about me?

The last lights of the town disappeared. She began to despair. It's my fault, she told herself. He thought I didn't care enough about Stefan, so he decided to do something about it.

She turned away from the car door, trying not to cry. She didn't know how she would manage alone. She didn't even know where the train was going. For all she knew, Ratface was setting up reception parties at every station along the line. And who was going to believe her story of imprisonment and mountain compounds and midnight escapes if there was no one to back her up?

The train settled into a steady, devouring rumble through the night. Christina walked unsteadily down the corridor, looking closely at every door. OCCUPIED. OCCUPIED. OCCUPIED. She imagined the people asleep in their bunks, ordinary people who couldn't begin to understand what had happened to her. If I knock on one of these doors now, she thought, and ask for help, they'll call the conductor and throw me off at the next town.

OCCUPIED. OCCUPIED. VACANT.

Vacant! Christina looked both ways along the dimly lit corridor. Nothing but the rhythmic swaying of the train. She opened the door slightly and peered in. The compartment was empty.

She slipped inside, turning the door latch to the OCCUPIED position. Then she stopped and thought: What if the conductor patrolled along there during the night? Wasn't it possible that he'd know which compartments were empty and which were occupied? She turned the door latch back again, crossed to the window to close the blind, and explored the cramped space of the compartment.

It was a twin-berth cabin. A long seat took up most of the space. Above it were instructions for releasing the two fold-down beds stored behind the wall panel. I'll sleep on the seat, she thought. I can't make any noise or leave any sign that I've been here.

A door in the opposite wall led to a tiny shower, toilet, and sink. She stepped through and stood for several minutes looking at her reflection in the mirror. People must know, she thought. They must look at me and know I'm not like normal kids. She peered more closely. Do I look different? She practiced making faces in the mirror. But it was no good. She was sure that an aura of difference hung about her, detectable by everybody she met.

She returned to the compartment, yawning. The clacketing wheels were lulling her into sleep.

Before settling down she opened a small cupboard door in the wall next to the shower. She was in luck: spare blankets, pillows, and towels.

Christina slept then, wrapped in two blankets, her head on a thin foam pillow. The wheels drummed along the rails, the headlight probed the darkness, people dreamed through the hours. Christina dreamed, too—of a rowboat beating uselessly through the waves, of a sad figure waving, receding.

But a part of her stayed alert, even as she slept. When the train slowed down later, she sensed it. She blinked awake, sat up, and looked at her watch. Three o'clock in the morning.

She opened a corner of the blind. They were approaching a town. She saw the smeary glow of streetlights in the morning mist, then platform lights, the station name—Kingston—and the yawning, bleary, sour faces of people who would rather still be in bed.

And Max.

And Ratface, with Stefan and Harvey Two in his arms.

They were peering at the car numbers. The train heaved, jerked, stopped. Christina didn't move. She sat, immobile, while the train waited. When it pulled out again a minute later, the platform was bare.

He's betrayed me, she thought. They're here. They're coming for me even as I wait.

She got to her feet and opened the door.

25

MAX WATCHED Christina advance along the corridor of Car 5. Her face was stony and cold. He swallowed nervously. She seemed to radiate waves of fury.

But she walked right past him. She stopped in front of Ratface and said bitterly, "Here I am, saving you the trouble."

Ratface smiled his rodent's smile. "Thank you, Olwen."

"My name is Christina," she hissed. She turned to Max. *"Kenelm.* How nice to see you. Feeling proud of yourself?"

Max had never seen her so angry. I must make her understand, he thought. I can't lose her now. "It's not . . . I didn't—" he began.

"Now, now, Olwen," Ratface said. "Don't be unkind."

"Uncle grabbed us at the station," said Max in a rush. "But the train left before he could get you."

Christina stared at him. Bit by bit, her anger was replaced by doubt. "Grabbed you? Didn't you take Stef to the doctor?"

"The doctor? No. We went to get Harvey Two. Stef left him behind in the car—"

Ratface interrupted again. "Enough of this. We don't want to wake other people. Olwen, were you alone in that compartment?"

"Yes."

"Good."

He began to push at their shoulders, guiding them back along the corridor to Christina's compartment. "No noise, please," he said, when they were inside. "No attracting anyone's attention. It's me they'll believe, not you."

Max compared their ragged clothes, their sleepy, wild, fugitive appearance, with Ratface's neat suit, smooth hair, and convincing manner. He's right, he thought.

He glanced at Stefan. Sleep and warmth at the Ellises' had restored him a little. He was looking up at Ratface with dark, mutinous eyes.

"Sleep," Ratface said. "That's what we all need. Kenelm, fold down the top bunk. Olwen and Arne will sleep there. You and I will sleep sitting up on the seat. Only four hours to go. No one will be wanting this compartment now."

"The names are Christina, Max, and Stefan," Christina muttered. "Anyhow, why don't you buy tickets for us and avoid all this secrecy?"

Ratface ignored her. He stood by the compartment door, watching them prepare for sleep. Max knew why Ratface didn't buy tickets. Ratface would always prefer secrecy to openness, and even though he looked respectable he didn't want to run the risk of being challenged by someone in authority.

The train beat on through the night, and, as heated air seeped in through vents in the floor, Max had a sense of isolation and insulation from the rest of the world.

When Christina and Stefan were settled on the top bunk, Ratface turned off all lights except the dim blue night-light. Max, slumped in the corner next to the window, felt the seat shift when Ratface sat down.

After a few minutes, Ratface began to speak softly about the League. Max tried to close his ears to the hateful voice, the ensnaring messages. It's false love, he thought. Everything Ratface says is wrong, even if he believes it.

Above him, Christina made exaggerated snoring noises.

When Max awoke three hours later, daylight was leaking in around the edges of the window blind. He heard knuckles rap sharply on a door farther down the corridor. A minute later, it was repeated, on a different door this time. There was also the rattle of dishes. Someone in a nearby compartment tapped a metal spoon on a cup. The passengers of Car 5 were being served breakfast.

Ratface jerked awake. For a moment, he looked fearful and uncertain. Then the expression vanished, and he moved to the door and put his ear to it.

Christina sat up, her face sleepy. "What time is it?"

"Shh," said Ratface warningly. He stepped away from the door. "It's half past six," he whispered. "At seven o'clock, if the coast is clear, we'll make our way to the restaurant car for breakfast, and stay there till the train gets in. No one will bother us there, but if we stay here, we're asking for trouble. Understood?"

Christina yawned and lay down again. Stefan coughed once and pushed back automatically into the warm curve of her body. He had woken and was staring malevolently at Ratface over the edge of the bunk. A funny kid, Max thought. He never speaks.

Christina opened her eyes. "What time does the train get in?"

"Nine o'clock," said Ratface.

"Gawd. A two-hour breakfast with you."

Max looked sharply at Ratface to see how he was reacting to this rudeness, but the leader of the

League was impassively combing his hair before the mirror on the door.

"We're going so slowly," Christina complained. "Where are we?"

Max opened the blind on the window and they looked out. The sun revealed itself as a dull gleam on the gray horizon. The train was hugging the side of a mountain, moving at a walking pace up a steep gradient. They were crossing a coastal range, he realized, for he could see a wedge of ocean far in the distance. Behind them curved the rear part of the train. Max looked down. The valley was deep, a network of black roads linking small farms and towns that were tucked among the folds of the earth.

Christina helped Stefan down from the top bunk. "More bloody mountains, no doubt full of scared White League families."

"Olwen," said Ratface sharply, "watch your mouth."

Christina's face was expressionless, but Max could hear her thinking: *Nya, nya, nya.*

At seven o'clock Ratface listened at the door, opened it gently, and looked out. "All clear. Olwen, you go first. Kenelm, you follow me with Arne. And no funny business."

They entered the creaking corridor and made their way down it in single file. On the floor outside most of the compartments were trays of finished and half-finished breakfasts. Scraps of toast lay on the plates. Tea slopped in some of the cups. An orange rolled across the floor, coaxed into movement by the slow rocking of the train. Max realized that he was very hungry.

At the end of the corridor was a door leading to the next car. At a right angle to it was the door through which passengers got on and off the train. This door was in two sections: the bottom half shut, the top half hooked back against the wall. Despite the slow pace of the train, cold air gusted through the opening.

"Wait," said Ratface softly, his hand on Christina's shoulder.

An elderly man stood at the half-door, smoking and looking out at the mountains. He turned at their approach, nodded hello, flicked his cigarette onto the tracks, and stepped through the connecting door to the next car.

When the man was gone, Ratface pushed Christina ahead of him again.

Then he made his first mistake.

Instead of following Christina into the next car, Ratface paused where the elderly man had been and looked out through the opening, his arms folded, his waist near the top edge of the half-door.

In that moment, he was defenseless. Stefan dropped Harvey Two, jerked free of Max, and charged, shouting incoherently. His small hands struck Ratface forcefully in the back. Ratface stumbled forward a little, his waist striking the top edge of the half-door.

He would have recovered his balance if Max hadn't finished the job. Max bent over and hauled upward on Ratface's skinny ankles. Ratface disappeared over the door like a diving clown in a circus.

No one else saw it happen. Max and Stefan stood there, looking back along the tracks. Ratface was a rapidly diminishing figure. His tiny, distant, futile arm waved up at them from the bottom of a thorny bank.

26

"*I THOUGHT* you were supposed to be following me," Christina said crossly, returning from the next car. "I turned around and no one was there. What are you looking at? Where's Ratface?"

Stefan looked up at her, his face alight. He pointed.

Christina joined them at the half-door. "What's going on?" She looked out, then back down the tracks. She put her hand to her mouth. "I don't believe it!"

"Stef pushed him," Max said, "with a little help from me."

"Stef! You didn't!"

Christina embraced Stefan, who smiled shyly. "My hero."

For a moment, Max felt a twinge of regret. Ratface had looked terribly small and pathetic back there. "Shouldn't we tell someone?"

Christina laughed disbelievingly. "Tell someone? Max, he's not dead. There are towns down there. Don't you see? We've made it. We're safe."

Max grinned uncertainly. "It was so sudden, that's all."

"I know," Christina said. She hugged Stefan again. "You saved us, Stef."

Stefan gave a short, barking laugh. "Got him,"

"Got him," Christina agreed. She turned to Max. "Let's wait in the compartment. I'd feel safer there."

They filed back the way they had come. As they passed the breakfast trays, Max said, "Are you two hungry?"

Christina nodded. "See what you can scrounge."

That's when the conductor of Car 5 finally noticed that all was not well in his domain. Max had just filled his hands with leftover oranges, toast, juice containers, and pats of butter when a man in uniform stepped into the corridor behind them and said, "What are you kids doing?"

He was a tall, stoop-shouldered, dandruffy man. He had shaved himself carelessly, nicking his chin but leaving a line of stubble along his jaw. He hated shaving, trains, and children—in that order.

"Well?" he demanded. Then he noticed the food. "Put that back at once."

Max tumbled the breakfast scraps onto two nearby trays.

"What are you doing here anyway?" the man asked. "This is for sleeper passengers only."

"We were going back to our car," Max said.

A cunning, self-important look passed across the man's face. "Let's see your tickets." He snapped his fingers. "Come on, come on. I haven't got all day."

The change that had come over Stefan was short-lived. He seemed to shrink from the size and the anger of the conductor. He turned his head into Christina's waist and began to weep and cough.

"You're scaring him," she said, glaring at the conductor.

Max was looking up and down the corridor. Could they make a run for it? The train was very long—plenty of hiding places.

"Well?" the conductor said.

Christina watched the man's stubbly face, formulating an explanation. Then she realized something quite simple: she no longer felt afraid. They didn't have to run or lie anymore. They were out of Ratface's reach. Getting into trouble for not having a train ticket was utterly unimportant. They were in the hands of the authorities now. When the train pulled in at nine o'clock they would simply ask someone to help them.

"We haven't got tickets," she said.

"You mean you've lost them."

"No, we never had tickets in the first place."

The conductor straightened his shoulders grimly. Stowaways. He'd never had a stowaway before. "That's an offense," he said.

Christina grinned at him. "Don't care."

"Don't care? You'll be fined. If I had my way, I'd put you in jail and throw away the key. How far are you going?"

Max felt buoyed by Christina's high spirits. "To the end of the line."

"Where'd you get on?"

"Blackwood."

"Blackwood?" the conductor said. "Don't tell me you skulked around the corridor all night?"

Max pointed. "We stayed in that compartment."

This was worse. Red patches appeared on the conductor's face. For a moment he couldn't trust himself to speak.

"We kept it neat," Max said.

"That's not the point," spluttered the conductor. "We don't want riffraff like you in our sleeper compartments."

Christina was becoming impatient. "The point is," she said, "we are here now, and we want help."

The train had reached the summit of the mountain. It began the slow descent to the city by the sea. As it picked up speed, the cars jerked and rocked.

Bracing himself, the conductor said, "Help? What kind of help?"

"We've been held prisoner by the White League. We escaped from them two days ago, and now we want to go home."

Even as Christina said it, the explanation sounded absurd.

Clearly the conductor thought so. He snorted irritably. "One thing I hate is a liar."

"She's not lying!" Max shouted. "We were held against our will. Then this little kid arrived and we felt sorry for him and escaped so we could take him home."

"*Two* liars," the man said.

People up and down the car were opening their doors, peering out, and jerking back again from the conductor's angry glare. Now and then, economy-class passengers edged past, making their way to the restaurant car for breakfast. We're wasting time, Max thought.

"We don't care if you believe us or not," he said. "We're prepared to wait quietly till the train gets in, then we want to see someone in authority."

"You'll see a policeman, that's who you'll see," the conductor said heatedly. Then he ran out of steam. What was he going to do with these brats? Perhaps he should tell someone about them.

He came to a decision. "Since you've already messed up that compartment, I want you to go in there, shut the door, and not say a word to anyone. Understand?"

"Gawd," Christina said. "Some sense at last."

She carried Stefan into the compartment, Max following her. As he closed the door on them, the conductor said, "I repeat: Stay here. I have to report this."

"Of course you do," said Christina.

He went out. Some time later they heard raised

voices in the corridor. "You can't go in there," the conductor said. "Just try and stop me," another voice said, and then the door sprang open.

The newcomer was Moaner's age, and large and soft like Moaner, but she had a strong face and it was expressing emotions they'd never seen in Moaner: outrage, solicitude, and impatience. She burst into the compartment, the conductor crowding in behind her. She wore a white apron over a pale blue dress and was carrying a cardboard box in the crook of her arm. They watched her set it down at their feet.

"Don't pay any attention to this clown," she said, jerking her head to indicate the conductor. "He likes to bully people. That's all he's good for. The name's Elsie," she said. She pointed at the box. "Eat."

There were ham sandwiches in the box, cans of Coke, chocolate bars. Max, Christina, and Stefan stared at her.

"Eat," Elsie said again. "You must be starving, poor dears. Did you sleep? Are you warm enough?"

Slowly, warily, they began to eat. Elsie hovered nearby, blocking the conductor, spreading her warmth over them. "Shut up, you old windbag," she told him.

Stefan grinned and pointed. "Windbag."

"You got it, sonny."

"Who's going to pay for all this?" the conductor demanded.

"I paid for it, okay? So shut up," Elsie said.

She smiled at the children. "Feeling better?"

They nodded. Here was another kind act from a stranger, and it gave them courage. There must be others like Elsie who will help us, Christina thought.

"What happened to you?"

They told her.

Elsie shook her head and clicked her tongue. "Terrible," she said. Then she looked at them with compassion. "I should be at work. Will you be okay?"

Christina said, alarmed, "We don't want to go back to the compound."

Elsie said firmly, "If you repeat that long enough and hard enough, they'll listen to you eventually." She softened. "Look, kids, it's out of my hands. I sell sandwiches and coffee—what can I do? Just hang in and demand what you want, okay?"

And she was gone.

Christina glanced at Max. There was a light in his eyes. Elsie had come and gone, full of energy and encouragement, sure that goodness existed in the world, and that they had a right to it. If she felt like that, so could they. An unspoken communication passed between Christina and Max: *We can do it.*

In the remaining ninety minutes of the journey, news of the presence of stowaways spread through the train. Christina, Max, and Stefan sat close together, their arms protectively around one another, enduring the stares and whispers of conductors, stewards, drivers, cooks, and engineers. Every few minutes, it seemed, the compartment door opened and a head appeared to scrutinize them.

But the stares and whispers were kindly, not hostile. Maybe there are more Elsies in the world than people like the hamburger man and the conductor, Christina thought. She smiled at the strangers. She liked sitting there, feeling Stefan's warmth against her, feeling Max's arm around her shoulders and her arm around his. There will be big changes soon, she thought. I may not see Stefan again, but what if I never see Max again? She didn't want to think about that possibility. But she'd been sharp and impatient with him in the past, and he might be glad to see the last of her.

"Max," she said hesitantly, "I hope we can see each other again, when all this is sorted out."

He turned to her. Strong emotions worked in his face. "Me too," he said. "Besides . . ."

He paused uncertainly.

"What?" said Christina, coaxing him.

"Nothing."

Christina brushed her cheek against his arm. "I understand," she said.

Did she? Max hadn't said a tenth of the things he wanted to say to her.

He turned away, staring through the window to hide his feelings. He saw that they had left the mountains and were on the coastal plain. For the past twenty minutes the train had been clacking smoothly through endless suburbs. He blinked. Is this where I was born? Will we find our families here? Will they want us? A few days ago, he realized, these questions would have overwhelmed him. Now he thought he could handle them, no matter what happened.

He realized that Christina was talking to him. "Max," she said, "tell me again what happened at Blackwood."

He turned away from the window. "We were going back for Harvey Two," he said. "Suddenly Ratface appeared."

"Yes, but how did he know we were in Blackwood?"

Max clicked his tongue in disgust. "It was hopeless from the start. According to Ratface, when we escaped in the car, Mr. Ellis woke up, ran out after us, and saw which direction we were heading. He phoned Ratface and Sergeant Hanley. While Hanley set up a roadblock on the other side of Blackwood, Ratface searched the town and spotted Mr. Ellis's car at the station."

"I thought you'd deserted me."

"No. Never."

"What happened after he grabbed you?"

"When he saw the train pulling out, he telephoned Slinger and Moaner, and then we drove like mad to get to Kingston before the train did. He was scared you might get off there. He was really worked up. He said we had to explore every last centimeter until we found you."

Christina looked away, considering what she'd just been told. Then she turned to him again. "Max," she said quietly, "why did he telephone Slinger and Moaner?"

Max had been remembering the wild drive through the mountains with Ratface. When he finally registered what Christina had asked him, the blood drained from his face. He looked at Christina in horror. "I've just remembered. He told them to pick us up at the end of the line."

27

CHRISTINA TOUCHED his arm. "We've still got a chance. Slinger and Moaner won't make a fuss if a lot of people are around. In fact, we'll make the fuss."

Max shook his head gloomily. "More running," he said, imagining their flying heels on the platform, the passengers scattering, the guards tripping over suitcases.

"Don't give up yet. There's always a chance. All we need is for one of us to get away. All we need is for one person to listen to us."

She looked out as if that person might be there, just on the other side of the glass. The train had slowed to a walking pace. They were on a broad delta of branch lines, passing grimy signal boxes, obsolete train cars, and messy stacks of iron rails. Workers tossed down cigarette butts as if gesturing in contempt at the train. Beyond the grubby rail yards, vast buildings poked into the darkening clouds.

Not a cheering start to the day.

The compartment door opened. Their conductor entered, rubbing his hands together. "We stop in one minute. You will then be escorted to the station authorities for questioning."

The light darkened. The train was drawing under the platform roof. The people waiting for the train began to smile, wave, or peer hopefully at every window. Christina looked. No sign of Slinger or Moaner.

A massive heave. The train had stopped. They waited.

Two minutes later the conductor was joined by three men. They were the kind who stand around with their eyes vacant, their mouths open.

"Gawd. They're trying to catch flies," Christina mocked.

Nothing. Not even a puzzled frown. The mouths remained open. No help from this bunch, Christina thought. She stood up.

"Not yet," the conductor said. "We wait till everyone has left the train and the platform is clear." He glared at her, as if he knew she was the one most likely to cause trouble. "We don't want to give you three any opportunity to create a disturbance."

Christina sat again. They waited for fifteen minutes. Perhaps Slinger and Moaner will think we're not coming, she thought. Perhaps they'll give up and go home.

"Right," said the conductor finally. "One at a time."

He stood back, allowing the three men to escort Max, Christina, and Stefan onto the platform. The fingers gripping Max's upper arms were like bands of iron. Christina struggled uselessly ahead of him. The third man held Stefan's hand, tugging on his thin arm, and when Stefan stumbled, swept him into bearlike arms and carried him.

"Let me go!" Christina shouted.

"Stop that," said her guard, shaking her a little.

"Why treat us like prisoners? We won't run away."

The guard ignored her. There was no one to hear her. Apart from a janitor and several abandoned luggage carts, the platform was deserted.

Max caught the eye of the janitor. "Help us!" he yelled.

"Kids," said the janitor disgustedly.

It was a long platform. Their progress down it seemed fateful, measured, as if they were being marched to their deaths. At the end of the platform they were taken through a gate and then on to an office. A sign said SECURITY. Stefan's guard knocked on the door. A voice called, "Come in."

They entered the office, bringing with them the

chilly air of the station. Notices flapped on the wall. A grim-faced man standing with his back to a small potbellied stove said sourly, "Shut the bloody door."

He was not alone. There were two other people in the room. They stood up as Christina, Max, and Stefan filed in, flanked by their escorts.

28

"*THIS THEM*?" said the man at the stove.

Slinger gave an apologetic nod. Moaner washed her hands together nervously. "We're terribly sorry to put you to all this trouble."

The man shrugged. "You've paid for their tickets, so let's leave it at that. But if it happens again, there will be a heavy fine."

"Yes. Of course," Slinger said.

The man nodded to the guards. "Wait outside."

The guards left the office.

"No!" Christina said. "Call them back. These people aren't our parents. They're holding us prisoner."

The official shook his head in irritation. "I'm not interested. You caused enough trouble already." He pointed to a radio transmitter. "I've been speaking on that bloody thing all morning. Be thankful your parents were here to meet you or you'd be in worse trouble."

Max hissed, "They're not our parents."

"I want my mother," Stefan said.

"In my time, I've heard every story in the book," said the man. "You'll have to do better than that." He turned to Slinger and Moaner. "I'm sorry, I'm very busy, you know. You're free to take your children and go."

He opened the door and they left the office. The three guards were waiting, their mouths open. Like puppets they fell into position and discreetly escorted the huddled family through the station to the parking lot. I can't believe this is happening, Max thought. No one's listening to us. No one's interested in helping us. We'll just have to fight the League ourselves. We've come too far to go back to the old way of life.

They reached the car. The guards stood back, watching Stefan and Slinger get in the front seat and Moaner get between Max and Christina in the backseat. They nodded abruptly, wheeled around, and returned to the station building.

Slinger steered cautiously out of the parking lot and onto the streets of the city. What an assault on the senses, thought Max, distracted from their predicament for a moment as he took in the hectic traffic, fumy air, and complaining horns.

Some time later the skyscrapers, taxis, and buses gave way to long, tired streets of shabby houses and apartment buildings. Far in the distance was the coastal range. Christina stirred.

"You'll never be able to hold us, you know. We'll escape again," she said savagely.

Moaner's hands began to twist together. "We— I—"

"So what are you going to do about it?" Christina went on. "Lock us up in a cell? Make things 'nicer' for us?" She sat back, her arms folded. "Even if we don't escape, we'll never cooperate. We think everything the League stands for is rubbish. From now on, we make up our own minds."

Moaner tried again. "Father and I have been talking—"

"Not interested."

After a while, Max sensed that Christina was trying to attract his attention. He leaned forward to peer at her past Moaner's bulk. She was frowning crossly as if to say, *Come on, help me.*

"Stefan—I mean Arne—is sick," he announced.

"His name is Stefan," said Christina, "and I'm not calling him anything else. And it's wrong to keep him from his real mother. She's the one who'll make him better."

"We think—" Moaner said.

A great wave of rebellion finally swelled in Max. "Think, think, think!" he burst out. "Ratface does all your thinking for you."

Slinger spoke for the first time. He took one hand from the steering wheel, picked up a scrap of paper, and peered at it. "Forty-eight Gore Street," he said. "Should be down here on the left."

He slowed the car. A hundred meters later he turned left into a narrow street between blocks of sun-blistered apartment buildings. A scruffy black cat twitched its tail in the weak sun, barely tolerating a group of children who were bouncing a tennis ball against a wall. Other children plowed plastic toys through banked sand in a sandbox. There were no adults about.

Christina sat forward suddenly. She grabbed Slinger's collar. "You can't! Not another one! You can't take another kid away!"

At that moment, Stefan seemed to jerk awake. He pressed his nose to the window of the passenger door. He was quivering. He's scared, Max thought. He's reliving the kidnapping.

But Stefan said one word, "Harvey!" Then, without warning, he opened the door of the moving car and tumbled out before anyone could stop him. He tripped, recovered, and ran to the cat. Slinger stopped the car. Even with the windows up, they could hear Stefan's joyful shout: "Harvey! Harvey!"

He clutched the huge cat around its stomach and heaved it toward cement steps that led to a faded brown door. He turned the knob, pushed open the door, and plunged inside.

Slinger started the engine again. He sat there

for a while, his hands on the steering wheel. "Uncle told us there's no love or goodness here," he said. "He was wrong."

Moaner finally found what she wanted to say. "We shouldn't have listened to him. We shouldn't have believed all the things he told us. I think we both knew it was wrong of him to take Stefan away from his mother, and that all three of you were unhappy, but we didn't know what to do—we had always listened to Uncle. I wish we'd been stronger—"

"When you escaped," Slinger broke in, "we saw Uncle's vicious side for the first time. It scared us."

"We'll help you find your own families now" Moaner said.

After a while, Christina said gently, "There'll be questions."

"We know."

They drove away in silence. Now and then Slinger brushed at his hair. Moaner wrung her hands. "It wasn't right," she said. "It just wasn't right."

Max and Christina, on either side of her, reached out together and stilled her troubled hands.